"I wish I hadn't come," Amber s

"What's wrong?" Nancy asked.

"Craig promised that he'd spend as much time with me as possible when he wasn't working," Amber said. "I don't even know what his job *is,* but I've hardly seen him. I confronted him earlier about it, but he just acted, well . . . *mysterious.*"

"Mysterious?" Nancy said. She remembered thinking the same thing about Amber.

The young woman nodded in response.

"Well, if there's a mystery involved, then Nancy is the one to talk to," George said.

Nancy Drew
Mystery Stories

Available from Simon & Schuster

NANCY DREW® 173

DANGER ON THE GREAT LAKES

CAROLYN KEENE

Aladdin Paperbacks
New York   London   Toronto   Sydney   Singapore

First Aladdin Paperbacks edition July 2003

Copyright © 2003 by Simon & Schuster, Inc.

ALADDIN PAPERBACKS
An imprint of Simon & Schuster
Children's Publishing Division
1230 Avenue of the Americas
New York, NY 10020

Printed in the United States of America

10 9 8 7 6 5 4 3 2

NANCY DREW, NANCY DREW MYSTERY STORIES, and colophon are registered trademarks of Simon & Schuster, Inc.

Library of Congress Control Number 2002115459

ISBN 0-689-86146-X

Contents

1

The Mysterious Woman in the Boutique

"Nancy! Nancy!" Bess Marvin called as she and her cousin George Fayne entered the Drews' house. "Where are you?"

At that moment Nancy Drew appeared in the doorway between the living room and the dining room, and she struck a model's pose. She was wearing a two-piece blue bathing suit that matched her eyes. Her reddish gold hair was piled on top of her head.

"Like it?" Nancy asked.

"Like it? It's *fabulous*!" Bess exclaimed. She was Nancy's age—seventeen—and had the same blue eyes, but Bess's hair was curlier and blonder than Nancy's.

"Is this your surprise? A new swimsuit?" George

asked. Although she and Bess were cousins, George had brown eyes and chestnut hair. Unlike Bess, who constantly struggled with her weight, George was athletic and had a lean and muscular build.

Nancy laughed and entered the living room. "Well, no—but it's part of it," she said. She plopped down on one of the plush sofas. "Have a seat and I'll explain."

Bess and George sat down across from Nancy. Nancy picked up a large manila envelope and shook the contents out onto the sofa beside her. "Three tickets for a Great Lakes cruise, from Chicago to Toronto. Dad's treating us!"

"All right!" George cried.

"Nobody can beat your father for great surprises, Nancy," Bess said. "What are the other ports of call?"

Nancy picked up the cruise line's brochures. "Sturgeon Bay in Wisconsin; Alpena and Port Huron in Michigan; and Lake Erie Beach in New York. When we get to Toronto, Dad is going to show us the sights."

"But why didn't you call us before, so we could all go shopping together?" Bess asked. "You know how much fun that is! And I could really use a new swim-suit. . . ."

"I know," Nancy agreed. "It just sort of happened."

"How so?" George asked.

"I was in Dad's office this morning when he told me that he was going to a convention of trial lawyers in Toronto. Then he told me that he had booked passage for the three of us on the SS *Great Lakes,* sailing from Chicago to Toronto," Nancy explained. "When I was walking back to where I had parked my car, I noticed this new boutique. It's called This Is Not Your Mother's Store. This swimsuit was in the window. I decided that I had to get it for thecruise. When I walked into the store, I found lots of other things I thought would be perfect. By the time I stopped shopping, I almost had a suitcase full of clothes!"

Bess put her hands on her hips. "Is there anything left for us to buy?" she asked with a grin.

"Plenty!" Nancy replied. "They were opening up new shipments when I left."

"Well, what are we waiting for?" Bess said. "Let's go!"

Nancy quickly changed into street clothes, told Hannah Gruen, the Drews' longtime housekeeper, that they were going shopping, and then they left the house. But just as they started to get into Nancy's car, a taxicab pulled up into the driveway behind them—and Ned Nickerson jumped out.

"Ned!" Nancy cried. "I thought you were in New York."

Nancy's boyfriend gave her a big hug. "I'm on my way to talk to some clients in Oklahoma City, but I was able to get a layover in River Heights," Ned said.

"I just had to see you, if only for a few minutes!"

Bess and George came over to join the reunion.

"How's the internship going?" George asked.

"Great," Ned said. "I think I may have a job with the company after it's over."

"Super," Bess said.

Ned handed Nancy a package. "This is for the cruise," he said.

Nancy gave him a puzzled look. "How did you know about that?" she said. "Dad only told *me* this morning."

Ned grinned. "Your father and I talk about all kinds of things," he said.

Just then the taxi driver honked his horn. Ned looked at his watch. "Gotta go. I can't miss the flight to Oklahoma City." He gave Nancy a big hug. "I'll call you later," he said.

Ned jumped into the backseat of the taxi. The driver backed out of the driveway and sped down the street.

"Oh, Nancy—that was so romantic of Ned. Just like in a movie!" Bess said. "Hurry! Open your gift. I want to see what he brought you from New York."

Nancy, still somewhat dazed by Ned's surprise visit, tore the brightly colored wrapping from the box. "It's Torino!" Nancy gasped.

"That perfume is so expensive!" Bess said.

"Ned probably can't even afford to eat now,"

George said. "Maybe you should send him a box of canned food."

"Oh, you two!" Nancy said. "Come on."

The three of them got into Nancy's Mustang and headed for downtown River Heights. Nancy found a metered parking spot just two doors down from the boutique, and she put in two hours' worth of coins.

"Uh-oh," George said as she surveyed the crowd of people inside the store. "I guess the word about those new shipments is out."

"We need to find Janine," Nancy said. "I told her I'd be back with two friends."

Janine was just finishing with another customer when Nancy and the girls located her. She gave Nancy a tired smile. "I had no idea our first week would be like this," she managed to say. "We've put in three frantic calls to the home office for rush shipments on several items in the store." She looked at George and Bess and added, "But we should still have your sizes in most things."

Nancy was impressed that Janine could just look at someone and know what size she wore. Everything she showed Bess and George fit them perfectly.

While Bess and George were looking at evening gowns, Nancy wandered over to a shelf of shorts and tank tops that she hadn't noticed when she had been in the boutique earlier.

Just beyond the shelf, standing at a rack of jeans,

were another salesperson and a woman whom Nancy calculated was in her middle twenties. She was very athletic-looking and had red hair and light freckles.

As Nancy was looking through the shorts for her size, she heard the woman talking about a cruise she was going on in a few days.

"I've never been on one before," the woman told the salesperson. "I have no idea what to take with me."

"Well, I've never been on one either," the salesperson replied. "I'd hate to sell you something that you wouldn't need."

Nancy didn't know if she should admit she had been listening or not, but the woman seemed genuinely lost as to what would be suitable for such a trip. She laid the shorts back on the shelf and walked over to the woman. "Hi! I couldn't help but hear what you were saying. My friends and I are going on a cruise in a few days too, and we're here to buy our wardrobes."

"Really?" the woman said. "Is it the SS *Great Lakes*, sailing from Chicago to Toronto?"

Nancy nodded.

"Great!" the woman said. She stuck out her hand. "I'm Amber Cosgrove."

Nancy introduced herself. "Those are my friends over there, looking at the evening gowns: Bess Marvin and George Fayne."

On hearing their names, Bess and George looked up and waved.

"If you'd like some suggestions, we'd be happy to help," Nancy said.

"Oh, I'd love that!" Amber exclaimed.

The salesperson who had been helping Amber seemed genuinely pleased too.

Nancy led Amber over to Bess and George, who were still looking at gowns. "Amber's going on the same cruise we are," she said, "and she wants some advice on what clothes to buy."

"Well! You're in luck!" Bess said. "If there's one thing I know, it's fashion."

"She's telling the truth," Nancy said.

Bess gave Amber the once-over, then pulled a midnight blue sheath off the rack and handed it to her. "This one, for sure," she said.

Nancy could tell it would make Amber look stunning.

"Why don't you try it on?" the salesperson suggested.

"Okay," Amber said.

Nancy and George also let Bess choose gowns for them, although Nancy admitted that she had already bought one earlier.

"Too bad. You should have waited," Bess said. "I can't imagine not seeing you in this pink strapless at least one night on the cruise."

After the other girls had finished choosing the evening gowns they wanted, they all headed for the swimsuits.

"You should see the one Nancy got, Amber," Bess

said. "It's blue, and it's just gorgeous on her! It brings out the color of her eyes."

Nancy blushed. "Oh, stop it, Bess," she said. She held up an emerald green dress. "Amber, this would look great on you!"

"Oh, yes, Amber!" Bess agreed. "Get it!"

Amber held it up against her and looked in the mirror. "I think Craig would like me in this."

Nancy looked at Bess and George.

"Craig?" Bess said.

Amber blushed. "Craig's my boyfriend. Actually, he works on the ship. That's why I'm going. He got me a special price on the ticket."

Suddenly, Nancy felt guilty. It had never occurred to her that perhaps Amber couldn't afford as many clothes as they were telling her she should get. What were they going to do? She didn't want to hurt Amber's feelings.

"Bess, if I get all the clothes that you think I should get, I'll clean out my bank account," Nancy said. "Maybe I should put some of them back."

Bess and George both gave her a confused look.

Nancy tried to catch their eyes to signal them not to say anything, but Bess didn't make the connection.

"Since when have you ever been on an allowance, Nancy Drew?" Bess said. "Your father would want you to take whatever clothes you thought you needed on this cruise."

Nancy glanced over at Amber, but Amber was

completely focused on some pants and tops. "What about these?" she said.

"Definitely," Bess said. "Perfect for when we're shopping on land."

For just a minute Nancy couldn't understand how Amber would be able to handle this huge clothing bill and be taking a cruise at a reduced rate. Then she realized that there was really nothing unusual about it at all. Anyone would jump at the chance to go on a cruise for a reduced price. For all Nancy knew, Amber had a good job and could afford a nice new wardrobe. Everything she took with her on the cruise she could use when she got off the ship.

Finally, everyone agreed that they had acquired perfect wardrobes for themselves and that there could never be four better-dressed women on any cruise.

As they prepared to pay at the cash register Bess groaned a little, saying that her father would probably make her wear everything for two seasons. Nancy noticed that Amber didn't flinch, though, when the salesperson told her how much her bill was. She paid with cash.

"This has been so much fun," Amber said.

"It really has," Nancy and her friends agreed.

"Is your car nearby?" George said. "Do you need any help with the packages?"

"No, I had the salesperson call me a taxi," Amber said. "I'll be fine."

While the salespeople finished wrapping the rest of Bess's and George's purchases, a cab pulled up in front of the boutique. Another salesgirl helped Amber load her packages into the trunk.

As Amber got into the backseat she waved to Nancy, Bess, and George, and then she mouthed, *See you on the SS* Great Lakes!"

The girls mouthed back, *Okay!*

As they headed to Nancy's car, loaded down with bundles, Bess said, "If the rest of the passengers on the ship are as nice as Amber, I'll never want the trip to end."

"Me either," George agreed.

But Nancy didn't say anything. She couldn't exactly explain it, but she felt there was something mysterious about Amber.

2

Amber's Strange Boyfriend

Nancy surveyed the pile of luggage that had been stacked at the entrance to the pier where the cruise ships docked on Lake Michigan—just east of downtown Chicago. "Are you sure we didn't forget anything?" she asked her friends with a wry smile. "There are only, let's see . . . forty or *fifty* suitcases!"

"If you're at sea," Bess said, "you can't just get in the car and run down to a store to get something you might desperately need!"

Nancy and George smiled at each other.

Just then one of the crewmen arrived with a flatbed truck to pick up the girls' luggage. Nancy noticed that some of the other passengers had started to board the ship.

The girls followed the crewman to the gangway.

The captain and some of the ship's staff were standing at the top, greeting everyone personally.

When the girls got to the top of the gangway, the captain gave them a big smile. "Good morning and welcome aboard." He shook her hand and offered Bess and George the same greeting. The girls introduced themselves.

A man next to the captain stepped forward and said, "I'm Eric Rankin, the cruise director, and this is one of my assistants, Adam Carson. He'll show you to your cabin."

"It's a pleasure to meet you," Adam said. He consulted a chart he was holding. "You have one of the suites on deck 5. This is deck 3. We'll take the elevator up. If you'll just follow me, please."

As they followed Adam toward the elevators Bess said, "Adam, does your list have the names of all the passengers?"

"It does, yes," Adam replied. "Were you wanting to know about anyone in particular?"

"Amber Cosgrove," Bess said. "What deck is she on?"

Without missing a beat, Adam checked the chart and said, "Amber Cosgrove, deck 5, cabin 525. It's just down the way, in fact, a couple of cabins past the elevators."

"Should we see if she got on all right?" George said.

"No, we need to unpack and find our way around the ship first. We'll call her later," Nancy said. "She may be with Craig now, anyway," she added in a whisper. "I don't think we should bother them."

When they reached their suite—number 502—Adam opened the door and held it so that Nancy, Bess, and George could enter.

"This place is huge!" George exclaimed.

"Our luggage is already here too!" Bess said. "That was fast."

Nancy noticed Adam smiling at them. "Will there be anything else?" he asked.

Nancy shook her head. "No, we're going to unpack and then take a look around the ship."

Adam consulted his watch. "You should have time to see most of it before the safety drill. That'll be on deck 3, about thirty minutes before we sail." He took a few steps toward the door. "If you think of anything else, just dial 43 for Guest Services," he said. "They're here to make sure you're as comfortable as possible."

"Oh, one more thing, Adam," Bess said. "When do we eat?"

Adam walked over to the door and showed them the schedule of mealtimes. "The restaurant is on deck 3," he said. "That's where all the main meals are served. You'll also find refreshment tables set up in the different lounges all over the ship."

"That sounds good to me!" Bess said.

"Believe me," Adam said, "you won't go hungry." He gave them a polite nod and left.

"We have three closets," George said as she began

13

unstacking the suitcases and placing them in front of the three closets. "This is great. We won't be climbing over one another when we're trying to get dressed."

"Nancy, there are two bathrooms!" Bess exclaimed. "You didn't tell me that."

"Actually, I didn't know until now," Nancy admitted.

The girls unpacked their belongings, looking over all of the great things they had bought in River Heights.

When they had finished, Nancy said, "Now let's check out the ship. We still have about an hour before we have to be on deck 3 for the safety drill. Let's start with the sundeck and work our way down."

They took the elevator to the sundeck, which was the next deck up. As soon as the doors opened, Bess saw the pool. "Our bathing suits are going to look great when we're lying out next to that pool."

"I'm going to be *in* the pool most of the time," George said. "I can't stop my training, even on this cruise, or I'll never make the swim team."

"Oh, George, give me a break!" Bess said. "There's no way you won't make the swim team."

From the pool area the girls headed to the fore-deck, where the Palm Garden Café was located.

"Hey—it's just like Adam told us," Bess said. "They have tables of food set up *everywhere*."

"Just looking at all that food is making me hungry," George said.

Nancy and Bess agreed.

14

They each helped themselves to a plate of fruit and cheese.

"I like this Great Lakes touch—I mean the fruit from Michigan and the cheese from Wisconsin," Nancy said, pointing to signs in front of each food item that indicated its origin. "It's fitting."

While they ate their snacks, they finished looking around the rest of the sundeck.

"I'm certainly not disappointed with what I've seen so far," Bess said. "I'm sure I'll be spending a lot of time on this deck."

They took the elevator down to their deck and walked along the corridor toward the stern of the ship. As they passed the library Bess said, "I certainly won't be spending much time in there."

"It's a great place to write letters and postcards," Nancy said.

"Now, here's what Bess is interested in," George teased as they neared a large circular room that was the ship's boutique. "Clothes!"

They went inside and made a complete circle of the store.

"Well, this stuff is nice, but I'm glad I bought my things in River Heights," Bess said.

"Yeah—I'd agree," Nancy said.

"What's on deck 4, Nancy?" George asked.

Nancy consulted a wall map. "A large lounge and the dance floor."

"I'm going to spend my days by the pool and my nights on the dance floor," Bess said, her mind clearly somewhere far away.

"I wonder if the pool stays open all night," George said. "I love midnight swims."

"We'll ask Adam," Nancy said. "Hey, here he comes."

Adam crossed over to where the girls were standing. "How's the tour going?" he asked.

"Wonderful," Nancy said. "We're really impressed with the ship."

"It's just two years old," Adam said. "It was custom built in Germany."

"How late is the pool open, Adam?" George said. "I'm in training for our school's swim team."

"Until midnight with a lifeguard," Adam said. "From midnight on, legally you're on your own."

Suddenly, a loud foghorn sounded.

Bess jumped. "What in the world is that?" she cried.

"I think that means it's time for us to return to deck 3 for a safety drill," Nancy said.

"That's it exactly," Adam said. "I'm your instructor, so I'll go down with you."

When they reached deck 3, they found a bunch of passengers who had gathered at the edge of the railings.

Adam introduced himself, then he issued everyone life jackets and demonstrated how to put them on.

"If there's a problem when we're on the water, this

16

is where everyone will gather. This is where your life jackets will always be," Adam told his group. "When you hear that same foghorn you heard a few minutes ago, you're to come here immediately. Don't go to your cabins to get anything. It's important that you remember that."

As Adam continued speaking Nancy thought he was doing a good job of explaining the procedures. He certainly seemed to be well qualified.

When the drill was over, Adam helped the passengers put their life jackets away. After that was done, everyone rushed to the railing to watch the ship pull away from shore.

Several people threw out streamers, but most people just watched the skyline of the city of Chicago get smaller and smaller.

"We need to go back to our suite and get ready for dinner," Nancy said. "This is our chance to show off our evening gowns."

As they headed for the elevators Bess said, "Look! There's Amber! Should we go say hello?"

Amber and a young man were standing at the railing near the stern of the ship. They looked like they were arguing.

"I wonder if that's Craig," George said.

"Me too," Nancy said. "If it is, we probably shouldn't interrupt them."

"Well, if that *is* Craig, it's not looking like Amber is

17

going to have a good time on this cruise," Bess said.

"We'll try to sit with her at dinner," Nancy said. "Maybe we can learn more about what's going on."

Once they were back in their suite, they showered and began dressing for dinner.

Bess tried on all three of her evening dresses before she finally decided on the red one. George tried on only one, but she kept groaning about how totally uncomfortable she was in it. Nancy knew which one she wanted to wear: the yellow one that reminded her of Hannah's daffodils. While she waited for Bess to finish dressing Nancy thought about what might be going on between Amber and Craig.

"We are absolutely gorgeous!" Bess said finally. "All eyes are going to be on us."

"Let's hurry so I can get back and get out of this thing," George said. "I really just want to try out the pool."

Bess shook her head. "I'm beginning to wonder if we're really cousins, George Fayne," she remarked.

They all took the elevator down to deck 3.

When they arrived at the entrance to the restaurant, Nancy quickly spotted Amber sitting by herself at one of the tables at the back of the room.

"We're in luck," Nancy said. She walked up to the maître d' to announce their arrival for dinner. "Nancy Drew, Bess Marvin, and George Fayne," she said.

The maître d' consulted his seating chart and told them that they were near the front of the restaurant.

"Do you see that girl over there?" Nancy whispered to him. "She's a new friend of ours, and we were wondering if we could sit with her. She looks so lonely."

"Well, I don't know, the seating chart is—"

Nancy cut him off. "Couldn't you switch us? She's not having a lot of fun."

At the mention of a passenger not enjoying the cruise, the man changed his tune. "It shouldn't be too much trouble."

Actually, it was no trouble at all. He merely punched some numbers into a computer, and in less than a minute the computer printed out a brand-new seating chart.

"Aren't computers great?" Nancy said to him.

The maître d' gave her a conspiratorial grin. "Yes, indeed," he said. He led the girls over to Amber's table.

When Amber saw them coming, Nancy noticed her face brighten for a split second. Very quickly, though, she went back to looking glum.

When the three of them were seated, Bess said, "This cruise is going to be so much fun, Amber! We took a short tour of the ship, and it has everything you could possibly want!"

"I wish I hadn't come," Amber said.

"What's wrong?" Nancy asked.

"Craig promised that he'd spend as much time with me as possible when he wasn't working," Amber

19

said. "I don't even know what his job *is*, but I've hardly seen him. I confronted him earlier about it, but he just acted, well . . . *mysterious.*"

"Mysterious?" Nancy said. She remembered thinking the same thing about Amber.

The young woman nodded in response.

"Well, if there's a mystery involved, then Nancy is the one to talk to," George said.

Amber looked puzzled. "What do you mean?" she said.

"It's no big deal, Amber. I always feel lucky when I can help people with problems like this, that's all," Nancy countered. She got embarrassed when people talked about her sleuthing. "If there's some way we can find out what the problem is, we'll be glad to help."

"Really?" Amber said. "Because . . . well . . . I don't think Craig told me the truth about who he really is."

3

International Fugitive

After breakfast the next morning Nancy went to the ship's library and searched the Internet for a list of the cruise staff. She wanted to find out a bit more about Craig.

Scanning the screen, Nancy saw that Craig was the assistant shore excursion manager. That meant he coordinated the activities of the passengers when the ship docked at the various ports of call.

Now Nancy was even more confused. *Why is it that Craig doesn't have enough time for Amber?* she wondered. Nancy was sure that Craig's busiest time would be when the ship was in port. When the ship was on the water, he'd still have work to do to make sure the passengers would have successful days onshore, but Nancy couldn't imagine that Craig was so completely tied up that he couldn't at least spend a couple of hours a day with Amber. Plus, he was the one who had asked her to come on the trip—and had even purchased her a ticket for less than the original cost.

Nancy knew that the reception desk was just past the elevators on deck 3. She decided that the best course of action would be to go there to ask about what kinds of tours were available when the ship stopped at Sturgeon Bay, Wisconsin. She was hoping that maybe Craig would be available to talk to her and that she could get a sense of what he was like from their conversation.

Unfortunately, when Nancy got to the reception desk, she saw that it was being manned by a young woman. Her name tag said SHEILA DOUGHTERY.

When Nancy told Sheila what information she wanted, Sheila said, "The shore excursion manager is in a meeting, but his assistant, Craig Oliver, is around here *somewhere*." Nancy could detect just a hint of disdain in her voice. It was obvious that Sheila didn't think too much of Craig's work ethic. Nancy was beginning to form a mental picture of him just from the little she had been able to glean from Amber and now Sheila—and she didn't particularly like what she was seeing. "I'd page him for you," Sheila continued, "but the last time I did that, he bawled me out."

"I think I know what he looks like," Nancy said.

She described the man she had seen Amber talking to right after they boarded the ship.

"That's Craig," Sheila said. She took a quick look around. "When you find him, you might tell him that you're the fifth person already this morning who's been looking for him!"

Nancy grinned. "I can probably work that in somehow," she said. "Any idea where I should start looking?"

"Well, he likes the sundeck," Sheila said. "Maybe he's there?"

"Thanks," Nancy said.

"I hope he gets in trouble," Sheila said, just loud enough for Nancy to hear.

"You never can tell," Nancy said.

Nancy took the elevator up to the sundeck. George had been swimming laps in the pool since breakfast that morning, and there was a crowd cheering her on. Craig Oliver wasn't part of the group, so Nancy continued her search, heading toward the Palm Garden Café. She entered by the fitness center and, not seeing Craig, exited by the pool bar. Just as she rounded the corner she spotted him. He was leaning up against a wall with his back to her.

What's he doing? Nancy wondered.

Suddenly, Craig turned his head. When he saw Nancy, he jumped.

Nancy decided to say nothing and keep walking.

She rounded another corner and almost collided with two men who also looked surprised to see her. They immediately hurried off.

Nancy stood where she was and looked at the retreating men. Right away she knew that Craig had been listening to their conversation and that she had interrupted them. Nancy walked to where Craig was still standing.

"You're Craig Oliver, aren't you?" Nancy said.

"That's what my name tag says, yes," Craig replied. "Why?"

"Do you always answer passengers' questions in such a hostile manner?" Nancy asked.

Craig took a deep breath. "I'm sorry, Ms. . . ."

"Drew. Nancy Drew," Nancy said.

"I'm sorry, Ms. Drew," Craig said. "You startled me, that's all."

"Did I interrupt your eavesdropping on the conversation those two men were having?" Nancy prodded.

Craig's face turned a bright red. "How dare you accuse me of something like that!" he said forcefully. "Who do you think you are?"

"Actually, I'm a friend of Amber's. She told me and my friends that you were ignoring her, after you went to all the trouble of getting her a reduced rate for this cruise," Nancy said. "So I was just doing a little detective work. That's all."

Nancy noticed a definite change in Craig's

demeanor. Now he seemed more confused than angry. "Did Amber put you up to this?" he asked.

Nancy shook her head. "No. I offered," she replied. "Amber said you were acting mysterious. I told her that I had solved some mysteries back home in River Heights, where my friends and I live. She asked me if I could help her solve this one."

Craig eyed her steadily. "And do you think you've solved it?" he asked.

Nancy shrugged. "Well, I caught you listening in on the conversation of a couple of the passengers," she said. "I don't think your superiors would be happy if they found that out." She paused for a minute to see if Craig would defend his actions. When he didn't, she added, "You'll have to admit that it looks suspicious. What were you trying to find out?"

Instead of answering her question, Craig said, "I'm curious, what gives you the right to go snooping around to solve mysteries in River Heights?"

"My father's a lawyer. He's worked on a lot of famous cases over the years that needed some detective work," Nancy explained. "That's how I grew up. I was surrounded by mysteries that needed solving."

"Then you'll understand that I'm not really eavesdropping on the passengers for my own gain, Ms. Drew. I'm doing some detective work too—for the ship. It's part of my job. Our final port of call is Toronto, Canada," Craig said. "I have to make sure that there is no suspicious activity on the ship that would in any way damage international relations." He smiled, thinking—Nancy was sure—that his explanation was more than sufficient for her. "So if you'll excuse me, I need to go about my work." He gave Nancy a slight nod and headed toward the elevators.

Now what? Nancy wondered. *What Craig said could be true, but there's something that's not adding up here.*

As Nancy circled back around to the pool area she noticed George getting out of the water to the applause of a sizable crowd. "George!" she called.

George dried herself off and came over to Nancy. "What's wrong?" she said. "You look like you're mad about something."

Nancy nodded. "I just met Craig Oliver. It's put me in a bad mood."

"I want to hear about it!" George said. She looked toward the huge refreshment table that was being set up on the other side of the pool. "But first let me get something to eat. I'm starved. Do you want something?"

"Not now," Nancy said. "But go ahead. I'll just sit here in one of the deck chairs and get some sun."

While George hurried toward the other side of the pool, Nancy sat down and closed her eyes. She could feel the warmth of the sun starting to penetrate her muscles and relax her.

"Ms. Drew?"

Nancy opened her eyes.

Craig was standing in front of her, blocking the sun. "May I join you?"

"Sure, why not?" Nancy said, acting nonchalant.

Craig sat down next to her. "What I'm about to tell you is in confidence," he began. "I just got off the telephone with my superiors at Interpol. Have you heard of us?"

Nancy was stunned. She sat up and looked at Craig. "Of course I've heard of Interpol. It's the International Criminal Police Organization."

Craig nodded. "Most of the countries in the world are member states," he said. "The national police groups of the different countries share information about worldwide crimes. We help one another catch criminals who cross borders."

"What are you doing on this ship?" Nancy asked.

"Before I tell you that, I also need to tell you that I discussed with my superiors the idea of asking you to help," Craig said. "In other words, I checked you out. And it looks like you're as famous as your father, the great Carson Drew."

Nancy smiled. "Why do you need my help?"

"I can't tell you everything right now," Craig said. "You'll just have to trust me."

"Do you have any identification on you?" Nancy asked.

Craig looked around to see if anyone else was watching them. When he felt the coast was clear, he pulled his credentials out of his pocket and opened them up for Nancy to examine.

"Looks real," Nancy said.

"They are real," Craig assured her.

"What's the gist of the problem?"

"What I told you earlier was true. Interpol is involved because this ship's final port of call is in Canada," Craig said, lowering his voice to a whisper. "Basically, we're trying to catch a fugitive who has robbed jewelry stores in Mexico and the United States of millions and millions of dollars' worth of diamonds."

Nancy cocked an eyebrow. "So you think that this fugitive is on this ship?" she said.

"If he's not now, he'll probably come aboard at one of the ports of call," Craig said. "We received a tip that the fugitive would be trying to escape to Canada this way. It made sense. Who'd think of using a cruise ship? I mean, after all, it's not the fastest way to get to Canada."

"You're right about that," Nancy said. She thought for a minute. "How do you know it's a he? Couldn't it just as well be a she?" she asked. "You know what they say: Diamonds are a girl's best friend."

Craig shook his head. "This time the song doesn't fit," he said.

"You seem to have a good part of this mystery figured out already," Nancy said. "How can I help you?"

Craig hesitated for a moment. "Well, some of this concerns Amber, whom I'm very much taken with, whether she believes it or not," he began. "I know now that it was a mistake to bring her along, but . . . well, I made the offer because I really do want to get to know her better. I think something very good can come out of this relationship. I'll admit it: I was being a bit selfish. I knew that I'd be working on this case, but I didn't want any other guy moving in on her."

"I guess I can understand that," Nancy said, "but, yes, asking her to come with you on a cruise and then ignoring her isn't the best way to start a relationship."

Craig smiled. "You don't have to beat me up about it, Ms. Drew," he said. "I've already been doing that myself."

"It's Nancy," Nancy said. "What do you want me to do?"

"Okay, Nancy. I'd like for you and your friends to continue to include Amber in your activities. Try to keep her attitude toward me positive. I'll do my part too. I'll try to spend more time with her," Craig said. He leaned over closer to Nancy's ear. "But when I'm with Amber, I need you to help me find the person responsible for stealing all those diamonds."

"Nancy?"

Nancy looked up to see George standing in front of her, holding a plate piled high with food. Craig had moved back away from Nancy, but she realized how strange it must have looked having him that close to her face.

"Great—you got something to eat," Nancy said.

"Yes," George said. She was looking at Craig. "Is this Amber's boyfriend?"

Craig stood up and nodded at George. "I sure am," he said, "and Nancy here has been giving me an earful!"

"Really?" George said.

Craig nodded. "She's been telling me how badly I've been treating Amber, and I've told her that's going to stop." He looked at his watch. "My colleagues will be wondering where I went." Looking directly at Nancy, he added, "I'm sure this is going to work out just fine."

Nancy returned his look. "I hope so," she said.

As Nancy watched Craig disappear it suddenly hit her: Someone on the ship could be an international jewel thief.

4

Nancy Investigates

Nancy took a piece of cheese from George's plate. "Let's see if Bess is up," she said.

As the two of them started toward the elevator George turned to her friend. "Is there something you're not telling me, Nancy?"

"Not exactly. Bess needs to be in on this too," Nancy replied. "I'll tell you two as much as I can."

There was a line at the elevator, so Nancy suggested they take the stairs. "It's just one deck down. We can get some exercise. Not that you really need it, after all those laps!" She smiled at George.

They found Bess in bed, doing her nails. "Well, I'm ready for another fabulous evening," she told them. She held up one hand. "Do you like this color?" she asked.

31

"It's too gaudy, Bess," George said. "Want some cheese and crackers?"

Bess shook her head and examined her hand carefully. "I think it'll work with the right lighting." She jumped out of bed. "Where have you two been?"

"George was doing laps, and I was having a very interesting conversation with Craig Oliver," Nancy said.

"Really?" Bess said. "I hope you let him have it!"

"Well, not exactly," Nancy said.

"Did I break up an important . . . conversation?" George interjected. "Tell us about it, Nancy."

"You didn't break up anything, George! Please," Nancy said. "Craig was explaining to me why he hasn't been seeing as much of Amber as he thought he would."

"Why?" Bess and George asked together.

"His job on this ship is just a cover. He's really a detective," Nancy said. "I can't tell you much more than that, except that I've been cleared to help him with the investigation."

"Cleared?" Bess said. "Hmm. Sounds like government work to me."

"Well, it's not the kind of government work you might be thinking of, but it does involve crossing international borders," Nancy explained. "Anyway, you'll just have to trust me."

"Okay," Bess and George said in unison.

The cousins were used to Nancy's having to be secretive sometimes about what she was involved in, to protect the integrity of the case. And they both knew that when everything was over, she'd let them know all the details.

"You'll be helping too, though," Nancy said, "with something very important."

"What?" George asked.

"Craig said the case is more complicated than he thought when he invited Amber to come on this cruise," Nancy explained, "so he wants me to help keep Amber occupied. He doesn't want her to be so lonely and thinking about why he isn't around. I'll need your help for that."

"Well, that should be pretty easy," Bess said. "I like Amber. There are plenty of things we can do together."

"Maybe she likes to swim," George added. "It would be easy to kill a lot of time in the pool!"

"I think we should play it by ear," Nancy said. "We'll probably have to do a lot of improvising."

"I have an idea," Bess said. She walked over to the telephone and rang Amber's room. "Hi, Amber, it's Bess Marvin. If you and Craig aren't doing anything now, let's go window-shopping! Okay . . . Great. I'll be there in half an hour." She hung up the phone. "I think I called at just the right time. I'm sure she'd been crying. She jumped at the chance to get out of the room." Bess shook her head. "I feel so sorry for her. She must be miserable."

Right then the telephone rang.

"I hope that's not Amber calling me back to cancel," Bess said.

Nancy picked up the receiver. "Hello. Oh, hi, Craig. What's up?"

"Meet me by the elevators in five minutes," Craig said.

"Okay," Nancy said. "I'll be right there." She hung up and told her friends what her short conversation was all about.

"He's not wasting any time putting you to work, is he?" George said.

"I guess not—but I did tell him I'd help as much as I could," Nancy replied. "I'll be back in a sec."

Craig was already at the elevators when Nancy showed up.

"I couldn't finish our conversation earlier because your friend came by," Craig said.

"I understand," Nancy said.

"There are three male passengers who fit the profile of a jewel thief," Craig began. He pulled a piece of paper from his shirt pocket. "I've written out their names and cabin numbers for you." He handed Nancy the piece of paper.

Nancy scanned the list, reading it aloud. "John

Fulcrum, deck 4, cabin 438; William Canton, deck 3, cabin 307; and Robert Jordan (married), deck 2, cabin 202." Nancy looked up at Craig. "What are these profiles you have?" she asked.

"Government agencies, including Interpol, have profiles for all kinds of criminals," he said. "These three men fit the bill for this jewel thief." Craig gave her a physical description of all three men.

"Amazing," Nancy said. "Okay, so what do you want me to do?"

"I can't tail these men everywhere. I have to work at my job sometimes to keep my cover, and I have to keep Amber happy," Craig said. "So I've figured out a plan. When I have to do something else, you'll take over. We'll use our cell phones." He handed Nancy a slip of paper with his number on it. "If you'll give me your number, I can call you and tell you when I need you. When I'm where I can tail these men, then I'll call you and tell you that you can stop for a while. I think it'll work."

Nancy wrote out her cell phone number and handed it to Craig.

"They've all pretty much settled into a routine," Craig said. "That's normal. Even jewel thieves fall into their own cruise ship routines. So that'll make it a little easier for us to decide when to be where. We'll sort of know what to expect from them."

"Okay," Nancy said. "I'll do what I can."

When she got back to the suite, Bess and George were ready for lunch.

"We're starving," Bess said. "You can tell us everything Craig said over lunch."

"That sounds good to me," Nancy said. "Wait a minute. I thought you and Amber were going shopping?"

Bess shrugged. "You hadn't been gone two minutes when Amber called and canceled. She said she had a headache. I'm a little concerned that she's still moping over Craig."

"Could be," Nancy said. *It's still a little strange,* she thought.

They decided the Palm Garden Café was the best choice for lunch, so they took the elevator up to the sundeck.

When the waiter had seated them at a table with a wonderful view of the distant Wisconsin shore, George asked about the meeting. "Well?"

Since she trusted her friends completely, and she felt she might need some help, Nancy decided to tell them that Craig had profiled three men on the ship as possible jewel thieves.

"Maybe I should put my bracelets and rings in the ship's safe," Bess said.

"I think he's pretty high-profile, probably not interested in the jewels of people on the cruise,"

Nancy said. "Plus, I doubt if he'd want to call attention to himself on the ship."

"Of course, it never hurts to be aware of the possibility," George added.

"True," Nancy agreed.

After their sandwiches arrived, Nancy finished telling them how she and Craig were going to handle tailing the suspects. "So if I get a telephone call and suddenly make an excuse to leave, don't say anything—especially if Amber is with us."

"You can count on us, Nancy," Bess assured her.

Nancy's cell phone rang just as she was about to open the door to the suite. The three friends looked at one another. Maybe it was Craig?

"Hello?" Nancy said. She listened for several minutes. "Okay. I'm on my way."

"So soon?" George said.

Nancy nodded. "Craig wants me to check on John Fulcrum. He's been making a number of cell phone calls in the lounge on deck 4, and I'm supposed to get close enough to him to hear what he's saying."

George and Bess went on into the suite while Nancy hurried to take the elevator down to deck 4. When she got to the lounge, she recognized John Fulcrum immediately. He was sitting at a table by himself, still talking on his cell phone. There were

37

several empty tables around him. Nancy sat down at one of the tables, took a paperback novel out of her purse, opened it up, and pretended to read. When the waitress came over, Nancy ordered a soft drink.

Mr. Fulcrum continued carrying on a conversation about buying and selling stock. Nancy listened closely for almost thirty minutes, but never once did she hear the word *diamonds* or anything else suspicious. Finally, Nancy decided that John Fulcrum was simply one of those men who liked to conduct business on his cell phone day and night.

Just as Nancy was leaving the lounge her own cell phone rang. It was Craig again, wanting her to see what Robert Jordan and his wife were up to. Craig was busy shadowing William Canton, and he had passed the Jordans on their way to the pool on the sundeck. "They were arguing about Mrs. Jordan's diamonds," Craig said. "I think it's worth looking into."

Nancy raced back to the elevator and rode up to the sundeck. The Jordans were sitting in deck chairs and were still arguing with each other.

Nancy made her way around the pool as unobtrusively as she could. Finally, she was almost behind the Jordans' chairs. She was acting like she was paying attention to a game of water polo in the pool, so as not to look suspicious.

"I need to sell those diamonds, Gwen. You don't need them," Mr. Jordan was saying. "We've already had this conversation."

"Why should you sell these when you have others you can sell?" Mrs. Jordan demanded.

Nancy was stunned by what she was hearing. *Could Mr. Jordan really be the man responsible for the jewelry store robberies in Mexico and the United States?* she wondered. *Could the mystery be this easy to solve?*

"Yes, I know that my mother willed them all to me and that there are others in the safety de—" Mr. Jordan stopped and looked directly at Nancy. "This is a private conversation, young lady. I'd appreciate it if you'd—"

"What? Stop watching the water polo match?" Nancy said. "It's a little difficult not to hear what you're saying, but since this is one of the best places to view the match, I'd prefer to stay. Please continue with your conversation, though. Rest assured that I have no interest in it."

Mr. Jordan seemed miffed. It was obvious that he wasn't used to being talked to like that. Mrs. Jordan, however, gave Nancy a grin.

After a few minutes the Jordans got up and moved to the other side of the pool. Nancy waited several minutes after they had left before moving, to make sure she didn't give them any reason to suspect her any more than they did. Finally, she headed toward the elevators. So far the investigation had yielded nothing. She decided to take a chance and call Craig. She knew his cell phone was on vibrate, so if he couldn't answer it, he wouldn't. He picked it up after a couple of rings, though.

"Nancy? I can't talk too long," he whispered. "What's wrong?"

"Nothing's wrong," Nancy said. "I just don't think either Mr. Fulcrum or the Jordans are the jewel thieves. What about Mr. Canton?"

"I struck out there, too. I'm beginning to think that maybe the fugitive hasn't come aboard yet," Craig said. "We dock in Sturgeon Bay tomorrow morning. I suggest that we still keep an eye on these three suspects, because of the profile—but the fugitive might also be one of the new passengers coming aboard in Wisconsin." He paused for a second. "Shoot—here comes Amber. I'll talk to you later, if I can." He quickly hung up.

When Nancy got to the suite, she immediately knew that Bess and George had something to tell her.

"What is it?" Nancy said.

"It's Amber," George said. "We just had a visit from her."

"Oh? I thought she didn't want to go shopping," Nancy said. "Did she change her mind?"

"Oh, she didn't come up here to go shopping," Bess said. "She thinks you and Craig are seeing each other secretly. She thinks you're trying to take Craig away from her!"

5

Suspicious Passengers

"Where in the world did she get an idea like that?" Nancy said.

Bess and George shrugged.

"I don't know, but she really believes it," Bess said. "She was really angry, too, and I think she has plans to do something about it."

"Oh, great," Nancy said.

"I kind of hope we don't see her at dinner tonight," George said. "It would be pretty sad if she made a scene."

Nancy took out her cell phone. "I'd better warn Craig," she said as she dialed his number. After several rings and no answer, Nancy hung up. "It may be too late," she said.

"Maybe we should go on deck and watch the fireworks!" Bess said.

"No thanks," George said. She wasn't a big fireworks fan.

"I'll tell you what we're going to do," Nancy said. "We're going to dinner tonight, and we're going to sit at Amber's table as if nothing has happened—and it hasn't, as far as Amber is concerned."

"Okay," Bess said. "I think I'll wear something old, in case Amber starts throwing things."

George laughed, but Nancy forced a half smile. She thought that something like that might be a definite possibility.

They needn't have worried, though. Later that night when they arrived at the restaurant, Craig met them outside the entrance and told them that Amber wasn't feeling well and wouldn't be at dinner.

"You know, she thinks you and I are seeing each other behind her back—romantically," Nancy said. "I have no idea where she got that idea."

Craig looked concerned. "I thought this instant sickness was a little weird," he said.

"You mean she didn't throw anything at you?" Bess asked.

"No, she just acted really tired," Craig said. "Now that I think of it, though, she wasn't too happy to see me. I thought it was just because she didn't feel well. . . ."

Just then Craig was paged over the intercom and asked to go to the reception desk. He told Nancy he'd talk to her later about what they would do when the ship docked at Sturgeon Bay the next morning.

The dinner turned out to be even better than the previous night's. A couple from Amarillo, Texas—the Lowes—was seated with the girls. Mrs. Lowe told them that they had asked to be moved from their other table to get away from what seemed like the most conceited couple in the world.

"I don't mind listening to other people talk about themselves," Mrs. Lowe said, "but when I talk about *myself*, I expect them to listen to me, too!"

"Makes sense to me," Bess agreed.

Over dinner Mr. Lowe told the girls all about life on their ranch in the Texas Panhandle. Several times he invited the girls to come out to see them. "We've got an airport in Amarillo that even has jets," he said. "You'd think you were in New York!" He gave them a big wink to show them that he was kidding.

When Nancy finally looked at her watch, she was shocked to see how late it was. "Well, I hate to break up this party, but I'd better call it a night," she said. "We reach our first port of call in the morning, and I want to be rested so I can enjoy it."

Everyone else agreed that it was time to turn in, so they all made their way out of the restaurant together. The Lowes had a cabin on deck 3—the same deck as the restaurant—so they said their good-byes to Nancy and her friends at the elevator.

"If you like to shop, you'll see me tomorrow, because that's what I'll be doing," Mrs. Lowe said. "Shopping until I drop!" She gave them a hearty laugh.

"I'm sure I'll see you, then, Mrs. Lowe," Bess said, smirking at George.

On the way up to their deck Nancy said, "I don't mind telling you I almost had an upset stomach thinking about what might have happened at dinner if Amber had showed up. But this turned out to be one of the best times I've had in weeks!"

"I agree," George said. "Maybe we should take Mr. Lowe up on his invitation to spend a couple of weeks on their ranch."

"Let's keep that in mind—maybe for next summer," Nancy said. "Right now I think we need to look over the Sturgeon Bay and Door County brochures to map out tomorrow."

Nancy woke up a couple of hours before her friends the next morning because she wanted to see Door County, Wisconsin, as the ship made its way into the harbor.

Door County, Nancy had read, had the look and feel of New England—one of Nancy's favorite parts of the country. The area was full of rocky coves, small fishing villages, and colorful cherry, apple, plum, and pear orchards. She was really looking forward to exploring the terrain.

Their ship had just started inching around the tip of the peninsula when her cell phone rang. It was Ned.

Nancy thanked him for the bottle of Torino, told him that he shouldn't have spent that much money, and then asked him how things were going in Oklahoma City.

"I've signed up the two clients I came to see, and I'm talking to two more this afternoon," Ned said. "They're going to love me back in New York!"

"Great, Ned!" Nancy said. "I am so proud of you."

They talked for several more minutes. Just before Nancy hung up, she told Ned that she was helping to investigate a mystery but that the girlfriend of the detective thought that Nancy was interested in the detective romantically.

"Well, I'll be glad to set her straight on that, if you want," Ned offered.

Nancy laughed. "No thanks. We can handle it! You just take care of your clients in Oklahoma City."

Just as Nancy ended her conversation with Ned, her cell phone rang again. This time it was Craig.

"We'll be docking in thirty minutes. Everyone on the crew has something he or she has to do," he said. He sounded like he was out of breath. "There's a place called the Sturgeon Bay Restaurant on the first street after you leave the dock area. I'll meet you there an hour after the ship has docked. We need to talk about the investigation."

"Okay, but what about Amber?" Nancy asked.

"She's still not feeling well this morning," Craig said. "She doesn't plan to get off the ship. She told me she was going to stay in bed all day."

"Well, that'll solve one problem, I guess," Nancy said, "but it still concerns me that she thinks you and I . . ."

"That's been taken care of," Craig assured her. "I had a long talk with her last night."

"Okay," Nancy said. "I'll see you at the Sturgeon Bay Restaurant one hour after the ship has docked."

Nancy was waiting at a table by the front window of the restaurant when Craig got there. She had already ordered lemonade.

"I thought maybe Amber had changed her mind about staying on the ship," Nancy said.

"No. I just had some extra chores to do before I could leave," Craig explained. "Sorry I'm a little late."

"So what's the plan?" Nancy asked.

"I'll continue to check out these three men, even though I'm starting to doubt any of them are our man," Craig said. "Still, since they fit the profile, I thought I'd see if they do anything suspicious onshore."

"That's probably a good idea," Nancy agreed.

"What I want you to do is check out any other suspicious activity among the rest of the passengers," Craig said.

"Even the women?" Nancy asked, one eyebrow raised. "I thought you didn't think the thief was a woman."

"I don't," Craig said, "but that doesn't mean a woman can't be an accomplice."

"Well, at least I can be with Bess and George," Nancy said. "I think they're beginning to wonder why they came on this trip."

"Good," Craig said. He looked at the half-empty lemonade glass. "I'll pay for that, if you want to go find your friends."

"Thanks," Nancy said. "I'll call your cell phone if I learn anything."

"Okay," Craig said.

As Nancy left she was struck by the same feeling she had when she first met Craig. She just didn't really like him, and she couldn't figure out why. Was it his treatment of Amber? Was it his attitude toward women? She couldn't put her finger on it.

Nancy knew where Bess and George were going first: the Apple Orchard, a shop on Main Street. The store sold all kinds of products made out of apples, including dolls with dried-apple heads.

When Nancy got there, Bess and George were looking over a shelf of dolls with faces that were all kinds of incredible shapes. It all depended on how the apple had dried.

"My mother has always wanted one of these. Her grandmother had one that had belonged to her mother," Bess said. "My mother saw it only a few times, but she said she could never get it out of her mind."

"It's amazing what artists can do with things from nature," Nancy said, holding an apple doll in her hand and looking closely at its face.

"Remember that kid in the tenth grade who painted faces on smashed aluminum cans?" George said. "I was always amazed at the faces he could see in them."

Bess wrinkled her nose. "Somehow I don't think this is quite the same thing, George!" she said.

George shrugged. "Art is art, Bess," she said. "It's in the eye of the beholder."

"Well, hello there!"

The three girls turned to see Mrs. Lowe and another woman, who was stunningly dressed.

"Don't they have some absolutely gorgeous things in here?" Mrs. Lowe said.

"Yes, they do," Nancy agreed.

"Oh, where are my manners?" Mrs. Lowe said. "Let me introduce my new friend, Laura Houston. Laura's from New Orleans. Her husband is in Argentina for a month, so Laura decided to come on this cruise."

Mrs. Houston extended her hand to all three girls. "It's a pleasure to meet you," she said.

"Now, that's somewhere I haven't been yet," Nancy said. "Argentina."

"Oh, I've been there several times," Mrs. Houston said. "I just didn't want to go this time because my husband went to the coldest part."

"It's wintertime down there now, isn't it?" George asked.

"Exactly," Mrs. Houston said.

"Isn't she wearing the most gorgeous outfit? I'd never find anything like that in Amarillo!" Mrs. Lowe said. "Everything matches. Even her fingernail polish!"

"Well, thank you," Mrs. Houston said. "I got this dress at a shop in New Orleans." She twirled around. "My husband will probably make me take it back when he gets the bill for it." She smiled, revealing teeth that almost sparkled. "Oh, well, I'll just tell him it's my birthday present or something like that."

"And that gold necklace you're wearing is absolutely beautiful," Bess said. "I love the design."

Mrs. Houston touched her neck. "I got this in Chicago before the ship left, and I'm getting rather superstitious about it too," she said. "I've had nothing but good luck since I put it on. I don't think I'll ever take it off!"

"Well, I want to see some of the other shops,"

Mrs. Lowe said. "We'll compare notes tonight at dinner, yes?"

Nancy, Bess, and George told her that they thought that was a great idea.

Nancy asked Mrs. Houston about joining them, but the well-dressed woman said that she didn't want to hurt the feelings of the people with whom she was already sitting.

Bess finally decided on a doll for her mother, then the girls spent the remainder of the day checking out the rest of the town's shops, cafés, galleries, and restaurants.

But Nancy didn't forget her promise to Craig: that she would keep an eye out for any suspicious activity. It was easy to do, since people had been asked to wear name tags to identify them as passengers on the SS *Great Lakes*. That way, they could take advantage of special offers from the Sturgeon Bay merchants. But Nancy noticed no suspicious activity whatsoever. All of the passengers seemed to be enjoying themselves immensely.

When it came time to return to the ship, the girls were very reluctant to leave.

"This is one place I want to spend some more time in," Nancy said. "Door County, Wisconsin."

"Me too," Bess agreed.

As they climbed up the gangway, Nancy's cell phone rang. It was Craig again.

"Two new male passengers are boarding the ship here," he said. "One of them could be our fugitive."

"Do you know what they look like?" Nancy asked.

"Not so loud," Craig said. "They're right behind you."

6

Bess's Accident

At Craig's warning Nancy stumbled and fell. While a concerned Bess and George helped her up, Nancy took a good look at the two men behind her.

The first man fit the stereotypical description of a mobster. Nancy tried to never stereotype people, but given that she knew the man might be the expected jewel thief, she couldn't help but wonder about him.

"Nancy!" Bess said. "Are you all right?"

"I'm fine," Nancy assured them. "It's nothing."

She let the first man pass them. Nancy was sure he had seen her fall, but he didn't offer to help in any way. She made a mental note of that.

The second man looked like a professional athlete. He was muscular and clean-cut. If she stayed with stereotypical descriptions, there was no way he could be the fugitive.

"Are you sure you're all right, miss?" he asked. "That was a nasty fall."

Nancy gave him a big smile. "I'm okay," she said. "My ankle just gave out on me."

The man returned her smile. "That's happened to me on the football field before," he said. "I'm Brad Snider. I play for—"

"I thought I recognized you!" George said. "You're going to be on this ship? Cool!"

George linked arms with Brad Snider and almost pulled him up the gangway, leaving Nancy and Bess looking at each other in amazement.

"I'm certainly glad I didn't really hurt my ankle," Nancy said, and laughed. "I'd still be lying there!"

"You probably need to have it looked at, just in case," Bess said.

Nancy linked arms with her. "There's nothing wrong, Bess. I fell on purpose," she whispered. "It was my way of getting a look at those two men behind us."

Bess stopped and gave her a look of admiration. "Nancy Drew, you never cease to amaze!"

"Oh, Bess . . . I wasn't checking them out!" Nancy said. "That was Craig on my cell phone. He must have been watching us reboard from one of the upper decks. He thought one of those men might be the fugitive he's looking for."

"Oh. Well, it can't be Brad Snider," Bess said. "Even I've heard of him."

"If I had to choose right now, I'd vote for the first guy," Nancy said. "He looks capable of robbing a lot of jewelry stores."

"Oh, you mean the one who just walked by when you were on the gangway and didn't say a thing?" Bess asked. "He *did* look creepy!"

"But we still need to keep an open mind about this," Nancy said.

Nancy and Bess found George and Brad at the elevators.

"Brad's on deck 4," George said. "After he's settled in, we're going up to the pool to do some laps."

"Well, that certainly sounds exciting," Bess said.

Nancy gave Bess a dirty look. "Don't be tacky," she whispered. "*I* think it sounds like fun," she said, turning to George and Brad.

When the girls were back in their suite, Bess fell into a chair. "Well, this is just great! Nancy's on a case, and George has a boyfriend. What happened to this wonderful trip we had planned to take *together*?"

"Bess! Brad's *not* a boyfriend," George countered. "He's a fellow athlete! He's going to help me with my strength training."

"Yeah, I'll bet," Bess muttered.

George chose to ignore her and began changing into her swimsuit.

"I may just go to bed," Bess said. "I'm pretty tired." She let out a big yawn.

"You're not going to bed. You and I are going to get dressed for dinner!" Nancy said. "After that we're going to the show. Tonight members of the crew are performing songs from some of the top Broadway musicals."

"Maybe," Bess said.

"No maybe," Nancy said. "You're going."

After George left, Nancy called Craig. He answered right away. Nancy filled him in on what she saw of the two men. "Brad Snider is a pro football player. He and George are swimming laps in the pool right now. I think we can forget about him," she said. "Do you know anything about this other guy?"

"Rudy Vincent. He's from Minneapolis," Craig said. "He deals rare books."

"You're kidding me," Nancy said.

"No, I'm not," Craig said. "And that doesn't mean he couldn't deal stolen diamonds, too."

"I suppose," Nancy said. "I'll keep an eye on him."

Nancy and Bess spent the next hour getting ready. They each tried on all of their evening gowns before choosing one for that night.

George called down to the room just as Nancy and Bess were headed out the door. She told them that she and Brad were going to eat in the Palm Garden Café but that they might see them later at the show.

Nancy repeated the conversation to Bess. When Nancy was finished, Bess said, "Sounds like a boyfriend to me!"

"Oh, Bess! You're so old-fashioned!" Nancy groaned. "Women and men can just be friends nowadays."

"Not if the man is as cute as Brad Snider, they can't!" Bess countered.

Nancy raised an eyebrow. "I think you're jealous," she said.

Bess glared at her for a moment, then burst out laughing. "Of course I'm jealous! I'm green with envy!"

When Nancy and Bess arrived at the restaurant, Nancy's cell phone rang. It was Craig again.

"Amber is feeling much better, but she's not letting me out of her sight. If I have a free moment, she expects me to be with her," he said. "She's also changed tables. Her excuse was that she met some really interesting people, but I think she's still jealous of us."

"Well, we'll deal with it, Craig," Nancy said. "Have fun. I'll check in with you later."

When they entered the restaurant, Nancy scanned the room. Her gaze fell on Rudy Vincent. He was seated at a table with several wholesome-looking couples, and he seemed to be completely enjoying himself. Nancy didn't think that the group was talking about stolen diamonds—and she was glad. She wanted to relax during dinner.

Both Nancy and Bess were happy to see that the Lowes were already at their table—and now so was Laura Houston.

Bess immediately brightened. "Oh, this is good!" she said. "But I wonder what Laura said to the people at her other table."

"I don't know, but I'm glad she's sitting with us now," Nancy said, "because it's certainly done wonders for your mood."

Bess smiled. "I'm sorry, Nancy. I was feeling kind of left out, I guess," she said. "But, yes—I really like Laura Houston. She seems like a great source of fashion information. I don't think I'd ever tire of talking to her about clothes."

"Well, hello!" Mrs. Lowe called to them. "Where's George?"

Mr. Lowe had stood up and was pulling out the girls' chairs for them.

"She's on the sundeck, swimming," Nancy said. "Her training is very important to her."

"One of the new passengers is Brad Snider, the professional football player," Bess said. "George and he have developed an instant *friendship*." Nancy noticed that Bess's hands made little quote signals when she said the last word.

After they were seated and had ordered iced tea, Bess turned to the newcomer at the table. "Mrs. Houston, I'm so—"

"Please, Bess, call me Laura," Laura Houston said.

"Okay. Laura!" Bess said. "I'm so glad you're at this table."

"Why, thank you," Laura said. "The people at my other table wanted to change too, so no one's feelings were hurt. I know I'll enjoy this table more."

"I have a lot of fashion ideas I want to talk to you about," Bess said. "I've been thinking about designing my own line of clothes."

Nancy looked at her. "Bess! That's a fabulous idea!" she said. "You never mentioned it before!"

"I guess I've thought about it over the years, although never seriously," Bess said. "But when I saw Laura just now, lots of ideas came to mind, and I thought, 'I can really do that!' You're a total inspiration, Laura."

"Of course you can design, my dear! That's exciting," Laura said. "I'd love to hear about your ideas."

The meal and the conversation almost made Nancy forget that she was involved in a huge case.

Time passed quickly, and before everyone knew it, dinner was over.

"Bess, I have decided that from now on I shall only buy my clothes from you," Laura said brightly. "I'm going to forget those New York and Paris designers!"

Bess blushed deeply. "Are you going to the show?" she asked her newfound friend.

"No, I had a very full day, and I'm tired," Laura said. "I like to unwind with a good book before I go to sleep, and I'm reading a wonderful mystery that has me totally stumped. I want to finish it tonight."

The Lowes said they were turning in too.

"We'll be in Alpena, Michigan, tomorrow," Mrs. Lowe said. "I hope it's as much fun as Sturgeon Bay."

Nancy and Bess said their good-byes and headed to the theater. George and Brad were waiting for them at the entrance.

"George is absolutely glowing," Bess whispered. "I've never seen her look like that."

"Exercise does that for you," Nancy said.

Bess looked at her. "Nan, I don't think it's the exercise that's causing it," Bess said. "I think it's Brad Snider."

The seats in the theater were on a first come, first served basis, and the theater was almost full by the time they found four seats together at the back.

Just as the curtain came up the man sitting in front of Bess straightened up. "I can't see now," she whispered to Nancy.

"Do you want to trade seats?" Nancy whispered back.

Bess shook her head. Nancy could tell that she had returned to the funk she had been in before dinner.

The first song had barely begun when a crew member from Guest Services handed Nancy a card. There was still enough light in the theater that she could read the message.

Nancy leaned over to Bess. "This is strange. It's a note from Craig," she whispered. "He says that Amber's not feeling well and wants to see me in her cabin right away. He says to please hurry and use the stairs instead of the elevator because they're closer." She sighed. "He's probably panicked because he doesn't have a clue about what to do."

Nancy started to stand up, but Bess put her hand on Nancy's arm. "I'm not really in the mood for this show, so why don't you let me go instead?"

"Are you sure, Bess?" Nancy said. "I don't mind."

"Nancy, I can take care of a sick person as well as you can," she said. "You're not the only one who's been a candy striper in a hospital."

"That's true," Nancy agreed. One of her favorite songs was just beginning. "Be my guest."

Bess slipped out of her seat and quickly left the theater. Nancy settled back to enjoy the music.

Two hours later the overhead lights came back on.

"George, we should go see if Bess needs some help with Amber," Nancy said.

"Okay," George said. Turning to Brad, she added, "I'll meet you at the pool at six A.M. We'll work some more on those breathing exercises?"

"Great!" Brad said.

When Brad was out of hearing, Nancy said, "Is there more to this than two athletes giving each other tips?"

"Nope. He's married with three kids. I even know their names, what they do at school, and that he's madly in love with his wife," George said. "He's also going only as far as Port Huron."

Nancy stopped and looked at her. "Really?"

George nodded. "It's a business trip. He's thinking about installing his personal fitness equipment on this ship," George explained. "His machines are already on several cruise ships that go from New Orleans to Jamaica."

"That's exciting," Nancy said. She was just about to ask George to give her some more details when a young man wearing a white hospital coat hurried up to her. "You're Nancy Drew, aren't you?" His name tag identified him as Billy Shannon, a member of the ship's medical team.

Nancy nodded.

"Your friend Bess Marvin is in the clinic," Billy said. "She slipped and fell going up some stairs. She twisted her ankle, but she's okay. She's resting comfortably now. I can take you to her."

Nancy and George followed Billy back to the clinic.

"When did this happen?" Nancy asked.

Billy looked at his watch. "A couple hours ago," he said.

"That was right after Bess left the theater," Nancy said to George.

George looked at Billy. "Why are you just now letting us know this?" she asked.

"Your friend didn't want to interrupt the show," Billy said.

Nancy shook her head. It was just like Bess to put her friends' happiness before her own.

Nancy and George soon arrived at the clinic and were taken to Bess's room. They found her sitting up in bed, watching a movie on television.

"How was the show?" Bess asked them. Her ankle was taped up, and it was elevated a bit. Nancy thought Bess seemed a little pale, but other than that, she didn't look the worse for wear.

"It was great, but I'm angry that you didn't have someone call us out," Nancy said. "Next time . . ."

"I'm fine," Bess protested. "They do want me to stay here overnight, though, because I also hit my head, and they want to make sure there's no concussion."

"What caused you to fall?" George asked.

Bess shrugged. "I was climbing the stairs that led

63

up to Amber's deck when I slipped. That's all I remember."

Nancy suddenly recalled Craig's explicit instructions to use the stairs instead of the elevator. "I'll be right back," she said.

Outside Bess's room Nancy found a wall map of the ship's deck plan. She easily located the stairs that Bess would have taken to Amber's cabin.

When she got there, a custodian was busy cleaning them.

"I think this is where my friend slipped and fell," Nancy said.

The custodian nodded. "Somebody spilled some really slick stuff on them. I don't know what it is, but it's been a real job getting it off," he said. "Is your friend all right?"

"Yes, thanks," Nancy said. "Is it safe to pass?"

The custodian nodded. "But hold on tightly to the rail," he said.

Nancy carefully climbed up the stairs and headed to Amber's cabin. She imagined that Craig and Amber had already decided that she wasn't interested in coming after all. Nancy doubted they had any inkling of what had happened to Bess.

Craig answered Nancy's knock. He looked surprised, then flustered. "What are you doing here?" he said.

Nancy gave him a puzzled look. "You sent for me.

Someone from Guest Services gave me your card, telling me that Amber was sick and that you wanted to see me right away."

"I'm not sick," Amber said. She had gotten up to stand behind Craig. "And Craig didn't send for you, either."

7

Locked in the Basement

Nancy left Amber's cabin and immediately headed to the reception desk on deck 3. She remembered that she still had the note that was supposedly from Craig. Bess hadn't taken it with her. Maybe someone in Guest Services could tell her something about who sent it.

A couple of girls who looked like college students were manning the desk when Nancy got there. Their name tags told Nancy they were Meredith and Rae Dawn. Nancy handed Meredith the note.

"This was supposedly from Craig Oliver, one of your employees—but he didn't send it," Nancy explained. "The message was a hoax, and I'd like to find out something about the person who left it."

"Nobody left it. It was a phone message," Meredith said. "I'm the one who took it."

"Then maybe you could tell me something about the person's voice?" Nancy said.

"I talked to a woman, not to Craig. She said that she was Craig's friend, Amber, but I knew she wasn't. Once I heard Amber and Craig talking at the reception desk, and Amber's voice was softer," Meredith said. "This woman was older. She told me to write that the message was from Craig because you might not come otherwise. I thought it was kind of strange at the time, but we're told to do what the passengers ask us."

"That's exactly the kind of information I was looking for," Nancy said. "Thanks. You've been very helpful."

As Nancy headed back to the clinic she was certain of one thing: Those slippery steps had been meant for her. Someone wanted to stop her. The person responsible for this had to be the fugitive that Craig was looking for—and she must be on his or her trail.

When Nancy got to Bess's room, she found George sitting in a chair, reading a magazine. Bess was asleep.

"What happened?" Nancy asked.

"They gave her something to make her relax," George said. She laid the magazine on the floor beside her chair. "Her ankle had started to hurt."

"Well, we need to talk. Let's head on up to the suite," Nancy said. "We'll leave word for the staff to call us if Bess needs anything."

"I've already told them," George said.

"Of course," Nancy said. "I'm not thinking clearly."

Nancy didn't say anything else until they were out of range of anyone in the clinic. "Those slippery steps were meant for me," she told George.

George gave her a funny look. "You mean it wasn't just an accident?"

Nancy shook her head. "No. Neither Craig nor Amber sent that note," she said. "I just got back from Guest Services. The crew member who took the phone message said she remembered Amber's voice from hearing her talk to Craig at the reception desk. This voice wasn't Amber's. She insisted that it belonged to an older woman."

"Is this connected to the mystery you and Craig are trying to solve?" George asked.

"I think it must be," Nancy said.

George took a deep breath. "So that means our nice, pleasant Great Lakes cruise has turned really dangerous?" she said.

"I'm afraid it does," Nancy said.

When they got to their room, Nancy called Craig. She was glad that he was back in his cabin so she could tell him what had happened. "You need to rethink who the fugitive is," Nancy told him. "There's a woman involved in this in some way."

"I still think our jewel robber is a man, Nancy. That's what the profile says," Craig insisted. "The woman could be his accomplice—someone who's just making sure he won't have any problems once he comes on board."

"Have you crossed Rudy Vincent off your list?" Nancy asked.

"Yes. He may look the type, but he's too busy doing other things, including playing cards," Craig said. "I don't think our fugitive is on the ship yet."

"Well, let's say that you're right about the fugitive being a man and that he hasn't yet come on board. I think a preemptive strike is called for here, though," Nancy said. "If we can discover who this female accomplice is, then maybe she'll be scared enough to give us the name of the fugitive—and then we can give it to the local police, who can stop the guy before he comes aboard."

"We're only picking up two passengers in Alpena, Michigan, tomorrow," Craig said. "They're both in their seventies. I think we can safely eliminate them."

Nancy didn't necessarily agree, because she knew a lot of people who were quite active at that age—maybe not in stealing diamonds from jewelry stores, but in other ways. But she decided not to say anything. Craig was in charge of the investigation, and he had already made up his mind.

"I think you need to be especially careful, Nancy," Craig said. "Whoever planned that first accident for you will probably try again."

"There are quite a few older women on this ship, Craig," Nancy said. "It'll be difficult to keep an eye on all of them."

"You don't have to do that," Craig said. "Just be suspicious of any woman who suddenly seems interested in being friends with you."

That was going to be difficult too, Nancy knew, because people tended to warm up to her. For part of the trip she would need to be a little more standoffish.

The next morning the ship docked in Alpena. Nancy scanned the town from the porthole next to her bed. It looked as interesting as Sturgeon Bay.

When Nancy didn't see George, she panicked—but she quickly noticed a note taped to the mirror.

I'm going to check on Bess, then Brad and I are going to swim some laps, George had written. *I'll be back in a couple of hours to go ashore with you. I'm taking Bess her sketchbook and a couple of drawing pencils.*

Nancy quickly dressed because she wanted to check on Bess too. She left George a note, telling her that she was going down to the clinic but would come straight back.

Bess was sitting up in bed, but she still looked uncomfortable.

"Well? How are you?" Nancy asked.

Bess let out a big sigh. "Okay. I just wish I could go ashore," she said. "Laura said there was a really great boutique here. I could probably get some more ideas."

"Laura has been here already?" Nancy said. "I wonder how she heard about your accident."

"I had quite a spill, Nancy," Bess said. "It's probably the talk of the ship."

"I guess that's right," Nancy agreed. "I wish there were something I could do."

"I'll be all right. My hand's not hurt, so I've been sketching a little," Bess said. "Laura's promised to come by after she's gone ashore and look at what I've done." She sat up some more. "Laura has a seamstress in New Orleans. She's going to have her sew up one of my designs, Nancy. Isn't that wonderful? I am *so* excited!"

"That's great news, Bess. I'm proud of you! I never knew you were so interested in designing," Nancy said. "Well, I wanted to check on you before George and I went ashore. You have my cell phone number if you need anything."

"Enjoy!" Bess said. She picked up a drawing pencil and made a few marks on her sketchbook. "I have something in mind that you might like wearing, Nancy."

Nancy grinned. "A Bess Marvin original," she said. "Can I afford it?"

Bess returned her grin. "You probably can *now*," she said, "but in the future, who knows?"

Nancy left Bess's room and hurried back to their suite. George had already showered and changed clothes and was waiting for her. On the way back to the room, Nancy had decided to take George into her confidence. There was too much danger for her

71

friends to be in the dark about what was going on. She told her friend the truth about Craig. "So it's a much more dangerous case than I originally told you," Nancy said.

"Wow!" George said thoughtfully. "This is a big operation."

"That's what I think too," Nancy said, "but sometimes I don't think Craig is up to it."

"Well, consider me a second set of eyes, Nancy," George said.

"Perfect," Nancy said. "Now let's go see what Alpena has to offer us!"

She and George headed down to deck 3. When they got there, Nancy saw Craig and Amber on their way down the gangway. Nancy pulled George aside. "Let's wait until they get to land," she said. "I don't want to start a fight between them."

"If I were Craig, I'd put an end to this relationship," George said. "Amber seems really high-maintenance to me."

Nancy shrugged. "Love does strange things to people," she said—but she agreed with George. Nancy honestly couldn't imagine this relationship going anywhere at this rate.

Nancy and George waited until Craig and Amber had disappeared down a side street before starting down the gangway.

"Where should we go first?" George asked.

"Let's do some window-shopping," Nancy said. "We can make a mental list of the shops we want to go in *and* I can do some detective work at the same time."

"So you're looking for an older woman?" George asked.

Nancy nodded. "Craig thinks she's the accomplice of the fugitive, and he doesn't think the fugitive is on board yet," she said.

"Does he think the person will board here in Alpena?" George asked.

Nancy shook her head. "Craig said the only new passengers are an elderly couple," she said. "He didn't think they were likely candidates."

"Well, there are only a couple more ports of call. Port Huron, Michigan, and Lake Erie Beach in New York," George said. "Do you think Craig is wrong about the fugitive escaping to Canada this way?"

"I'm not sure. As you said, there are still two more ports of call," Nancy said. "I think we'll just have to wait and see."

As Nancy and George window-shopped along Alpena's streets Nancy kept an eye out for older female passengers meeting with nonpassengers. When they had finished walking along what could be considered the "touristy" streets, though, Nancy hadn't seen anyone who wasn't doing the same thing she and George were: shopping.

The girls had a light lunch at the Alpena House,

then continued their circle of the downtown area.

"Oh, we're back at one of the shops I wanted to duck into, Nancy! The Thunder Bay Tea Room and Gift Shop," George said. "Let's see what they have."

The Thunder Bay Tea Room and Gift Shop defied description. Its stone walls were large and thick, and in between them the girls found every imaginable kind of ware.

"I could spend hours in here," George said. "I wish Bess could have come."

"She'd love it, wouldn't she?" Nancy agreed.

"Isn't this place incredible?"

Nancy and George turned to see Laura Houston smiling at them. "I haven't been anywhere else," she said. She had several packages in her hand. "I can't seem to get out of here. I'll buy some things and tell the clerk that's it, then I'll spot something else I have to have."

"Sounds like this place is a trap," Nancy said. "Maybe we should leave right now."

George shot Nancy an incredulous look.

"I was just kidding," Nancy said, smirking.

"You won't believe what's downstairs either," Laura said. "Things down there are even more interesting because they're from the town."

"Oh, that's what we want, Nancy," George said. "There's no sense in buying something you could get anywhere."

"Well, I'll see you back on the ship," Laura said. "I'm going back now so I can visit with Bess."

"She'd love that," Nancy said.

After Laura Houston left them, Nancy and George found the stairs leading down to the basement.

When they got to the bottom of the steps, they stopped and stared in amazement. First of all, the main basement room was huge—but Nancy could also see that there were various other rooms opening off the main room.

Nancy looked at her watch. "We don't really have all that much time, George, so we'd better get started."

Slowly but surely, they made their way through the room.

"We're the only ones down here, Nancy," George said. "I wonder why that is?"

Nancy shrugged. "Maybe the other customers don't know it's here, or maybe they've found everything they want upstairs."

As Nancy and George passed one of the smaller rooms, Nancy saw some shell jewelry that looked really interesting. "Let's look in here. Normally, this can be cheap and tacky," she said, "but I think this person knows what he or she is doing."

They worked their way toward the back of the room, where several exquisite necklaces were displayed. Nancy had just picked up one to examine it when she heard the door to the room slam shut.

Nancy looked at George. "I wonder how that happened," she said. She put the necklace down and went over to the door, a rush of panic beginning to creep up her spine.

The door wouldn't budge.

"Let me try," George said. She gave a run at the door and hit it with her shoulder, but it still wouldn't open.

"Let's use my cell phone," Nancy said. She took it out of her purse and was just starting to dial when she saw LOOKING FOR SERVICE flash across the display. "Oh, great! No service. It must be these thick walls."

George started banging on the door. "Help! Help!" she shouted. She turned to Nancy. "We'll miss the ship if we can't get out of here."

"I know," Nancy said. "And if you're not on board when it leaves, no one looks for you."

8

The Real Laura Houston

All of a sudden, the door clicked open, revealing a startled elderly man.

"How did you two get in here?" he demanded.

"We were just looking around, and the door shut on us," George said.

"It must have been a draft," Nancy said. "Sorry. We're going to miss our ship if we don't hurry."

"There's no draft in here!" the man shouted at them as Nancy and George raced toward the front entrance to the store. "This building is as solid as the Rock of Gibraltar!"

In the distance they heard the ship's horn sounding.

"Oh, George!" Nancy shouted. "It's leaving!"

George picked up her speed, leaving Nancy a few paces behind. "I'll stop it!" she shouted.

They finally had the ship in sight, but the gangway was being pulled up.

"Stop! Stop!" George screamed. Both she and Nancy started waving their hands.

At last one of the crewmen saw them, shouted something to the men on the shore, and the gangway was lowered back to the ground.

Nancy and George reached the gangway, raced onto the ship, and fell against one of the railings.

"You're lucky one of the crew saw you."

Nancy managed to look up, in between gasps for air. The captain was giving them both a stern look.

"We got locked in a room in the basement of one of the shops," George told him. "We didn't do this on purpose."

"Well, try not to cut it so close next time," the captain said. "We have a schedule to keep."

With that, he and one of his officers resumed their conversation.

Nancy was slowly getting her breath back. She looked over at George, who didn't seem to have been fazed at all by the run to the ship.

"Come on, George. I'm worried about Bess," Nancy said. "We need to go check on her."

"Why are you worried about her?" George said as they hurried toward the clinic.

"Getting locked inside that room was no accident," Nancy explained. "Someone did that to us deliberately."

When the girls reached the clinic, they discovered that Bess had been discharged a short time before and had gone back to their suite.

"She's managing quite well on her crutches," the nurse told them. "In fact, she probably won't even need them in a few days."

Nancy and George raced back toward the elevator and took it to deck 5.

They found Bess propped up in her bed.

"Thank goodness!" Bess cried when she saw them. "When your cell phone didn't answer, I thought something had happened to you. Especially after what I heard."

"What did you hear?" Nancy asked.

"Well, the clinic released me right before the passengers started reboarding the ship," Bess explained. "I was just about to go around a corner so I could take the elevator to our deck when I heard Craig and Amber laughing about something." She paused. "At first it sounded sort of like a romantic thing, if you know what I mean, and I didn't want to interrupt them. So I stopped. I thought Craig might be giving her a kiss. Instead, I heard Amber say something like, 'That should take care of them!' I was hoping to hear more, but they started walking again. They came around the corner where I was standing, so I had to pretend that I was adjusting my crutches."

"Craig and Amber?" George said. She looked over

at Nancy. "Do you think they're the ones who locked us in that room?"

Nancy told Bess what had happened. "My cell phone didn't work because of the thick walls," she said.

"I never trusted Craig," Bess said. "I think he's been treating Amber really poorly."

"Bess, you just said that both Craig *and* Amber were laughing about what happened," George said. "That means Amber knows about it and was probably in on it."

"Well, I'm quite sure that Craig talked her into it," Bess insisted. "I can't imagine that Amber would think up something like that on her own." She turned to Nancy. "Just how much do you know about him, Nancy?" she asked.

"Well, I . . ." Nancy paused. "I told George the whole story this morning, so I might as well tell you. Craig isn't just a detective. He works for Interpol, and he's trying to catch a fugitive who stole millions of dollars' worth of diamonds from jewelry stores in Mexico and the United States. This person is trying to escape to Canada."

Bess looked at her incredulously. "On a cruise ship?" she asked.

"It actually makes some sense, Bess," Nancy countered. "Because, just like you, most people would find it hard to believe."

"Did Craig show you his credentials?" Bess said.

"Of course he did," Nancy said.

"Did you study them carefully?" Bess said.

"Yes, I . . . well, I looked at them," Nancy said. She knew she was blushing. She hadn't really examined them carefully. "But, no, I didn't do any sort of test on them, if that's what you mean."

Bess just looked at her for a moment.

"Okay, so I probably let the thought of getting involved in an international mystery temporarily cloud my judgment," Nancy admitted. "I probably wanted to believe he worked for Interpol."

"Craig could be the fugitive himself, Nancy," George said. "Amber could be his accomplice."

"Or maybe Amber is his innocent victim," Bess countered. "I just really don't see Amber being involved in this."

"I think you're both wrong about Craig, but I'll do some research," Nancy said. "Maybe I'll call Dad in Toronto and ask him if he can find out about any investigation of jewelry store robberies in Mexico and the United States."

"That's a good idea. Makes me feel better," Bess said. "So tell me everything that you did in Alpena."

"Maybe later? I'm all talked—er, *shouted* out," George said. "I don't feel like using my voice. Why don't you tell us what you did?"

"Well, I designed some dresses for Laura, so

they'd be ready for her to look at when she got back on the ship," Bess said. "But I guess they released me before she could come by."

"That's strange," Nancy said. "We saw Laura right before we got locked in, and she said she was on her way to see you."

Bess shrugged. "Maybe she got involved with something else," she said. "I'll call her."

"Go ahead," Nancy said. "I want to take a shower."

"I need to do some laps," George said. "That'll help me unwind." George slipped into her swimsuit and left the suite.

Nancy undressed, put on her robe, and began brushing her hair. Bess picked up the telephone and called Laura's room.

"Hi, Laura. It's Bess!" Bess said. "The clinic discharged me before you got back on the ship. Did you find anything interesting in Alpena?"

Bess listened for a minute, then said, "Well, I have some designs I'd like you to look at, if you have some time. Could you come to our suite? We're on deck 5, suite 502." She paused for a moment, listening. "Okay. See you in half an hour."

Just as Nancy started to go into the bathroom she noticed that Bess looked suddenly glum.

"What's wrong?" she asked.

"I'm not sure," Bess said. "Laura's voice . . . she just didn't seem as interested as she was last night." She shrugged. "Well, she's coming—so I must be imagining things."

"She may just be tired, Bess," Nancy said. "She really was in a good mood when we saw her onshore, and she was looking forward to seeing your designs."

Nancy stayed in the shower longer than she normally did because it felt so good. By the time she got out and had combed her hair and brushed her teeth, Bess was in the middle of showing Laura her dress designs.

"Hi, Laura!" Nancy said.

Laura turned and smiled, then returned to looking at Bess's designs.

After several minutes Bess said, "Well, that's it. That's my collection. What do you think?"

"It's nice. You draw well," Laura said. "I'm just not sure anything here really appeals to me."

Nancy saw Bess's face drop. In fact, Nancy was a bit confused too. Laura didn't seem as friendly as she had been before, even when Nancy and George encountered her at the shop—and she certainly was not as lively as she was at dinner.

"I have some other ideas," Bess said. "I'll start on them right away, then show them to you."

Laura stood up. "Okay, if you want—but only if you feel like it. Now I'd better go. I have a million things to do!"

After Laura had left their suite, neither Nancy nor

Bess said anything for a few minutes. Then Nancy climbed onto Bess's bed and said, "Let me see your designs."

Bess pushed them over to her without saying anything.

"Bess, these are wonderful!" Nancy said. "So professional! I really can't believe there was nothing here that Laura liked."

"They were all designed with her personality in mind," Bess said. She paused for a minute. "It's almost as if—well . . . as if that woman weren't Laura."

Nancy stopped looking at the designs and looked at Bess. "What do you mean? Of course that was Laura. But maybe she was just tired, like I thought." When Bess didn't say anything, Nancy said, "What makes you think she's like a different woman, aside from the mood shift?"

"Well, for one thing, she wasn't wearing the gold necklace that she said she'd never take off," Bess said. "And another thing: Her fingernail polish didn't match the outfit she was wearing."

Nancy was amazed at Bess's observations. She hadn't noticed these things at all.

Suddenly, Nancy wondered if perhaps Bess might be right. Could the person who just left their room be an impostor?

9

Thief on Deck

"You've always been a good judge of character, Bess," Nancy said, "so if you think that woman wasn't Laura Houston, then I'm listening."

"Nancy, with the exception of the fingernail polish and the missing gold necklace, she *looked* like Laura Houston," Bess said. "She just didn't *act* like her." She shivered and pulled the bedcovers up around her. "It was weird."

Nancy used her cell phone to call Craig. "We need to talk now," she said. "It's very important."

Craig told Nancy that he was at the reception desk. He wanted her to pass by the desk without stopping; she should just walk in front as though she were on her way to someplace else. He'd follow her.

"I'll be back in a few minutes, Bess," Nancy said.

She thought for a minute. "Don't let anyone else in. If they knock, don't answer. George has her own key, so she won't need you to open the door for her."

"You're scaring me, Nancy," Bess said. "Do you think Laura is capable of doing something violent?"

"I don't know what to think, Bess. This really may be some elaborate hoax," Nancy said, "but then again, it could be the same Laura Houston—just a different version of her."

Bess gasped. "Do you mean she might have multiple personalities?"

Nancy shrugged. "I'm just saying that we should be prepared for anything, that's all." She went over and gave Bess a big hug. "Will you be all right?"

Bess hugged her back. "Yes, but hurry, okay?"

"Okay," Nancy said.

When Nancy got to deck 3, she actually had to fight a crowd to make her way to the reception desk. She wasn't sure how Craig would see her, but she continued past the desk. In a few minutes he caught up with her.

"Now, what was it you wanted to tell me?" Craig said.

"My friend Bess doesn't think Laura Houston is the same person who left the ship in Alpena," Nancy said.

Nancy could tell that Craig was caught off guard by that bit of information. "Who does Bess think she is?" he asked.

"She doesn't have a clue, but I've been thinking that perhaps it's related in some way to the diamonds," Nancy said. "There could have been a switch—maybe identical twins or something like that. This *new* Laura might be the one behind the robberies."

Craig shook his head. "Nancy, we've been through this before," he said. "I just don't believe that the fugitive is a woman."

"Don't you think we should at least keep an open mind about this, Craig?" Nancy said.

"Okay, okay," Craig said. "Why does Bess think the *new* Laura isn't the *old* Laura."

"Well, for one thing, her personality just seems different. She's not as lively as she was a day ago, not as vivacious," Nancy said.

"Maybe she's just tired," Craig said. "Cruises aren't for everyone, you know."

"Bess also noticed that Laura wasn't wearing a gold necklace that she said she'd never take off," Nancy continued, "and she had on fingernail polish that didn't match her outfit."

Craig gave her a blank stare. "I'd be laughed out of a courtroom if I tried to present that as evidence."

Nancy could feel her blood beginning to boil. "Nobody said anything about using it as evidence, Craig," she managed to say, "but sometimes it's the little things that give a criminal away—so it's never wise to ignore them."

"I think you're wasting your time," Craig said. "I think we still need to watch the men on the ship." With that, Craig turned around and walked away.

Infuriated, Nancy decided not to return immediately to their suite. Instead, she took the elevator up to the sundeck to see what George was up to.

George had just climbed out of the pool and was toweling off.

"I need to talk to you," Nancy said.

They found a couple of secluded deck chairs and sat down. Nancy told her about Laura's strange behavior and about Craig's thinking that there was nothing wrong with it.

"I hate to side with Craig, Nancy," George said, "but he may be right."

"Why do you say that?" Nancy asked.

"Laura might have talked to her husband in Argentina and gotten irritated about something," George said. "Or maybe Laura really wasn't serious about Bess's designs, and she's just trying to let Bess down gently."

"But Bess's designs are wonderful," Nancy said. "I think that anyone would—"

"Nancy, you think Bess's designs are wonderful because you and Bess are friends. And Bess's designs really may be great for the right person," George interrupted, "but maybe they didn't really appeal to

Laura. After all, you heard her say that she was going to stop buying from designers in New York and Paris and start buying from Bess. A little extreme, right? That honestly sounded to me like someone who was just trying to be nice."

Nancy took a deep breath. She wasn't used to such insightful comments from George. "All right—I feel a little foolish," she said. "You're probably right."

"Wait here. I need to tell Brad something," George said. "I'll be right back."

Nancy watched as George hurried back over to where Brad was talking to some other men. When George reached him, she squatted down by his chair and said something. Brad looked over and waved at Nancy, then George stood up and hurried back over. She grabbed Nancy's arm. "Let's go. Brad's busy talking to some men about investing in his cruise ship gym equipment," George said. "Besides, I'm beginning to feel guilty about spending so much time with him and so little time with you and Bess."

"I think we're both guilty of deserting her," Nancy agreed. "Let's turn this back into three best friends going on a Great Lakes cruise!"

When Nancy and George got back to the suite, Bess was dressed. "I was just about to come see what had happened to you," she said.

Nancy apologized, then told Bess what had transpired with Craig.

"Well, I think he's wrong," Bess said. "I was here with Laura, and I know that something isn't right."

"Bess, you can't just assume that—," George started to say, but Nancy interrupted her.

"I think we should just forget about everything except what we came on this trip for: rest and relaxation," she said. "I've always wanted to sit in a deck chair, facing a railing, and read a book—just like pictures of people on those old ocean liners that used to cross the Atlantic."

"Read a book?" Bess said. "I was thinking of something a little more exciting."

"I think relaxing in a deck chair, letting the cool lake breezes blow around me, and just thinking about the upcoming swim trials at school would be great," George agreed.

"I see I'm outvoted," Bess said, smirking.

The three of them each packed a canvas bag with their things and headed toward the elevators. Nancy and George were amazed at how well Bess could maneuver on her crutches.

They took the elevator to deck 3; it was the widest deck and had plenty of deck chairs. They found three together at the corner, where a cross corridor met the main deck, and made themselves comfortable.

Nancy stretched out and opened her book. When she looked over at Bess and George, she saw that they seemed to be enjoying themselves. George had closed her eyes, and Nancy was sure she was in the middle of a daydream about the final swim team trials. Bess had a smile on her face. Nancy hoped Bess was dreaming she was in New York, watching some famous models parade her fall collection down a runway in front of fashion editors and buyers from the biggest department stores in the country.

Nancy read a few more pages before closing her eyes herself and letting the lake breezes cool her face.

When Bess screamed, it took Nancy a few minutes to remember where she was.

"What's wrong?" Nancy gasped.

"My bag is gone. It had my purse in it!" Bess cried. "Somebody stole it!"

Nancy and George quickly found that their canvas bags were where they had left them.

Nancy looked around. "I know how it was done," she said. She walked to the corner. "Someone was hiding here"—she pointed around the corner—"and reached out and took your bag, Bess. It was the one on the end, so it was the easiest to take."

"What are we going to do?" Bess said. "It has all my money and . . ."

"Well, at least we know the thief can't have left the ship," Nancy said. "Let's go to the reception desk and report the loss."

They were already on the same deck as the

reception desk, so they hurried there as fast as Bess's crutches would allow.

Just as they rounded a corner Bess shouted, "There it is!" Sure enough, Bess's canvas bag was sitting on top of the counter.

No one was manning the desk, but there was a bell to ring for service. Nancy hit it with her palm.

Meredith appeared through a door that was obviously some kind of office. "Hi!" she said brightly. "What may I do for you?"

"This is my bag!" Bess said.

"Oh . . . all right," Meredith said. "Did you want to leave it here . . . or something?"

"No, it was stolen from me!" Bess said. "And I want it back."

It was obvious to Nancy that Meredith didn't have a clue as to what was happening.

"Did you know this bag was here on the counter?" Nancy asked.

"No, I've been doing some paperwork in the office," Meredith explained. "Rae Dawn is sick, Sheila has transferred to another area, and I'm totally behind. I put this bell out here so passengers could ring it if they needed service."

"So you didn't see how this bag got here?" George said.

Meredith shook her head. "Sorry."

"Okay, well, it does belong to Bess," Nancy said,

"and it was stolen just a few minutes ago from her while we were relaxing on deck."

"Oh, I see. That's horrible!" Meredith said. She looked around. "I'm not quite sure what to do in this case, since the bag's here."

"Don't worry," Bess said. "I'll just take it, and we can forget about it."

"You'd better look inside and see if everything is still there," George said.

"Good idea," Bess said. She rummaged through the bag, checked her wallet for missing money and credit cards, and then, finding nothing gone, she said, "Oddly enough, it's all here."

"Good!" Meredith said.

Nancy could see the relief on her face. "I guess we'll let you get back to your paperwork," she said.

Meredith gave them a big smile, then returned to the office.

As they started back toward the elevator Nancy said, "We were lucky this time."

"I'm not so sure," Bess said.

George looked at her. "What do you mean?" she asked.

"Nothing's missing, but everything is all messed up," Bess said. "It's obvious that somebody went through my things—looking for something."

10

Craig Is Missing

"Why would someone go through my things and not take anything?" Bess asked. "Especially since I had a lot of cash and credit cards."

"The person clearly didn't want any of that," Nancy said. "Whoever did it wanted to find out about you."

George turned to her friend. "What do you mean, Nancy?"

"Someone on this ship knows that he—or she—is being watched," Nancy explained, "and they want to know more about who's doing the watching."

"Why didn't they take *your* canvas bag, then, Nancy?" Bess asked. "You're the one who's most involved."

"Opportunity," Nancy said. "Your canvas bag was the easiest to get to."

"You mean there's still a chance that someone will try to steal *our* things too?" George said.

"Exactly. It's very important that we try to act as normal as possible," Nancy said. She thought for a minute. "We don't want whoever did this to know we suspect why it was done."

Bess and George agreed with Nancy that that was the right idea.

In keeping with their plan, the girls had dinner as usual with the Lowes and Laura Houston. When Nancy, Bess, and George arrived at the restaurant, though, it was as if they had traveled back in time a couple of days. Laura seemed to be in a really good mood again.

Nancy shrugged. "It may turn out to be a personality disorder after all," she whispered. "I say we keep an eye on her."

By the end of the evening, after everyone decided to turn in for the night, Nancy felt Laura Houston was just back to her old self.

As they headed out of the restaurant Bess said, "Well, were we wrong or what? She really must have just been tired when I talked to her earlier. I'm sure everything we thought about her can be explained."

"You're probably right," Nancy said.

The next morning, after the ship docked in Port Huron, Nancy, Bess, and George spotted Laura going down the gangway.

"I wonder if she'd mind if we tagged along," Bess said.

"Let's ask her," Nancy said.

"Come on! We'll lose her if we don't hurry," Bess said, "and I can go only so fast on these crutches."

The girls left the ship and in a few minutes were close enough for Laura to hear George's call. "Laura! Wait up!"

Laura slowly turned around and gave the girls a big smile. "Well, this is a surprise! I thought I was going to have to see Port Huron by myself."

"You don't mind if we tag along?" Nancy said.

"No," Laura said. "Why should I?"

"What happened to the Lowes?" Bess asked.

"They're meeting friends here in Port Huron," Laura said. "They're going to be busy all day." She gave the girls another one of her dazzling smiles. "I don't know why it didn't occur to me last night to ask if I could attach myself to you. I guess I just thought three young people wouldn't want to hang around with someone old enough to be their mother."

"Goodness!" Bess said. "I'd never think of you as my mother."

Laura blinked, then grinned. "Well, I guess that's a compliment."

Bess blushed. "I just meant that you . . ."

"I know what you meant, Bess," Laura said. She

locked arms with her. "I'm glad you want to spend the day with me."

Nancy had to admit that she was somewhat disarmed by Laura's charm—although some niggling doubts had begun to creep back into her mind about this woman. It was going to be hard to remain objective, she knew, but it was very important that she do so. Something wasn't quite right.

As the women strolled through the downtown streets of Port Huron, Nancy tried to keep the conversation going. She wanted to see if Laura might betray a hidden agenda. Two hours into their window-shopping, though, Laura had said nothing out of the ordinary.

"Let's have lunch at the Edison Inn," Laura said. "I'll buy."

"Oh, you don't need to do that," Nancy protested.

"I know I don't, but I suggested it. I'm getting hungry," Laura said. "Bess can talk to me some more about her designs over lunch."

Bess stopped and looked at Laura. "Are you really still interested in them?" she asked.

"Of course I am," Laura said. "Whatever gave you the idea that I wasn't?"

George glanced at Nancy and raised an eyebrow.

When they reached the Edison Inn, a waiter showed them to a table by the window that looked out on the St. Clair River.

"This table has the best view of the Bluewater Bridge and downtown Sarnia, Ontario," he told them. "You can also see the freighters passing by."

"Wonderful," Nancy said. "Thank you."

For a few minutes they admired the view, then they made their selections from the menu.

"Laura, I've been meaning to ask you something," Bess said. "What happened to your necklace?"

Laura blinked, seemed flustered for a moment, then put her hand to her throat. "Oh, you mean that gold necklace?" she said. "Well, unfortunately, it caused me to get a rash on my throat! I decided that I'd better not wear it anymore."

"I rarely wear jewelry myself, for that same reason," George said.

"I love that color of fingernail polish," Nancy said. "What do you call it?"

Laura looked at her nails. "Mountain raspberry," Laura said. "It's such a delicious shade, don't you think?"

"I've noticed how your fingernail polish always matches your outfits," Nancy continued, "so I was really surprised the other day when you came back on the ship in Alpena and it didn't."

Laura looked at all three of them for several seconds, then started laughing. "I suddenly feel as though I've been taken down to police headquarters for questioning," she said. "What's going on?"

"We're just very much aware of fashion!" Bess said, smoothing the waves.

"Yes," George chimed in. "You have such great taste that we just can't help but notice everything you wear."

"Honestly, though—we *have* been spying on you!" Nancy said. "We were trying to help Bess learn as much as possible about what you like to wear so she can design a wardrobe that you just can't resist."

"Oh, that is so sweet!" Laura said. She patted Bess's hand. "I feel bad about not paying more attention to your designs. Right after I talked to you, some personal problems came up, and that's all I could focus on."

George kicked Nancy under the table to remind her of what she had said previously—but Nancy was well aware of it. This whole situation with Laura Houston was like a roller coaster.

Their lunch came, and the conversation turned from fashion to food. Laura told them about the New Orleans recipes that she liked to use. She made the dishes—and the whole city—sound so appetizing that by the time they were having dessert and coffee, Nancy and her friends had decided that a trip to New Orleans was in order.

Nancy glanced at her watch. "We need to get back to the ship," she said. "If we're late again, I don't think the captain will be too happy."

Laura looked puzzled. "Late *again*?" she said. "When were you late before?"

Either Laura knew nothing about the incident in Alpena, Nancy thought, or she was a great actress. She quickly recounted what had happened in the shop after Laura had left them.

"Oh, my goodness!" Laura exclaimed. "That's terrible!"

"Anyway," Nancy continued, "we made it back to the ship just in time."

Laura looked at the check the waiter had left. She then took several bills out of her purse and laid them on the table.

On the way back Nancy thought about how the day had gone. Now she was even more puzzled than before. She'd talk to Craig about it later tonight. There was still something about Laura that concerned her. Nancy felt she had always had good instincts about who might or might not have committed a crime, but Laura Houston was someone she couldn't get a read on.

As she followed her friends up the gangway Nancy saw Amber talking to the captain. She looked very distressed.

"Something must have happened," Bess said.

"Yeah," George said. "Amber certainly looks upset."

"Do you know that girl?" Laura asked.

Nancy nodded. "We met her in River Heights," she said. "She's friends with one of the crew members."

"Well, I hope nothing serious has happened,"

Laura said, turning to leave. "It was a wonderful day, and I'm glad we spent it together. I think I'll head to my cabin now and rest a bit before dinner tonight. I'll see you then."

"Thanks again for lunch," Nancy said.

"Yes," Bess added. "That was so nice of you!"

Laura smiled at them. "The cruise isn't over," she said. "I'm sure we'll have some more fun times together."

When Laura was gone, the girls hurried up to where Amber was standing. She was still talking with the captain.

"What's wrong, Amber?" Nancy said.

"It's Craig," Amber said. "He's disappeared!"

11

Amber's Confession

Nancy couldn't believe what she was hearing. "What do you mean he disappeared?" she said.

Amber wiped her eyes with a tissue. "I need to sit down," she said.

"Why don't you go to the lounge on deck 3?" the captain suggested. "It's very close."

Nancy knew where the lounge was; they had passed it many times on their way to the restaurant. She led George, Bess, and Amber that way.

Nancy focused on this new development. She was sure that Craig's disappearance had something to do with the investigation of the diamond robberies. Before she made any decision about what she should do next, though, she needed to hear Amber's version of the incident.

Nancy was glad to find that no one else was in the lounge. They sat on a couch near the door so she could hear if anyone else was coming in.

"Quick, Amber—the ship is supposed to leave in just a few minutes. Tell me what happened," Nancy said. "Maybe we can still locate Craig."

"Oh, don't worry, Nancy. Craig's not going to be on this ship when it leaves Port Huron," Amber said. "He's gone because he doesn't love me anymore."

Nancy looked at Bess and George.

"How do you know that?" George asked. "Did he tell you?"

"Well, he didn't have to, did he?" Amber said angrily. "You know he didn't pay any attention to me on this cruise." She looked at Nancy. "I owe you an apology. I thought you and Craig had started seeing each other—but I know I was wrong."

"Right—Craig and I weren't seeing each other," Nancy said. "I *did* have several conversations with him, but they were about his work, not about you."

Amber blinked. "What do you mean?"

"I'll explain later," Nancy said. "But tell me what happened."

Amber told them that she and Craig had gone to a restaurant in downtown Port Huron. Craig had seemed preoccupied about something. When Amber asked him about it, he just got angry and told her it had to do with his job. He didn't want to talk about it.

They had eaten their meal in silence, but right before dessert came, Craig excused himself to go to the men's room—and never returned. Amber even had one of the waiters check the men's room, but Craig wasn't in there. She paid the bill and hurried back to the ship to tell the captain what had happened.

Just then the ship's horn sounded, and the lounge began to vibrate as the engines started.

George and Bess looked anxiously at Nancy.

"That's all, Amber?" Nancy said.

Amber nodded. "All my things are on this ship, and I don't know anyone in Port Huron," she said, "so I just decided to come back here and worry about what I'm going to do later."

"That creep!" Bess said. "I never trusted him."

Nancy subtly laid a hand on Bess's arm, to remind her not to say much else.

"What did the captain say when you told him?" Nancy asked.

Amber made a face. "Well, he was angry," she replied. "He said he'd report the disappearance to the Port Huron authorities. I could tell by his attitude, though, that he thought Craig really left just to get away from me."

Nancy didn't know what to do. If she said too much about her relationship with Craig, she'd jeopardize the investigation he was involved in; that is, if there really *was* an investigation. Could it be that

Craig Oliver was the real impostor on board? Nancy couldn't afford to take a chance by revealing what Craig had told her he was doing—at least, not until she did a little more investigating herself.

"Bess, why don't you and George see that Amber gets back to her cabin safely?" Nancy said. "I need to go back to our suite for a few minutes."

"Come on, Amber," Bess said. "We'll take you to your cabin."

"I know this has been a shock," George added, "but you have three friends here you can count on."

Nancy quickly headed toward their suite to phone her father. When she got there, she looked in her address book and found the telephone number of the hotel in Toronto where Mr. Drew was staying.

Nancy tried to use her cell phone, but she couldn't get it to ring the Toronto number. She picked up the receiver of the suite's telephone and asked the ship's operator to make the call.

Carson Drew answered on the third ring. "Nancy, it's so good to hear your voice!" he said. "You almost missed me. I was just about to leave for a meeting."

"I'll be quick, Dad," Nancy said. "I have something I need you to do for me."

"Sounds mysterious," Carson Drew teased. "I thought you'd be able to relax on this trip."

Nancy laughed. "I seem to attract big cases, Dad," she said. "You know that."

"I most certainly do," Mr. Drew said. "What is it that you need?"

Nancy quickly told her father everything she could remember about Craig Oliver and his investigation of the multiple jewel robberies. She told him about Bess's fall on the stairs and how she thought it had been meant for her, and about being locked in the building in Alpena. Nancy also told him about Laura Houston.

"But now, Dad, I'm not sure of anything. It could all be a hoax," Nancy said. "Can you find out if there really is an Interpol investigation and if the lead investigator is a Craig Oliver?" She gave her father a complete description of Craig so that she could be sure—even if there was an ongoing investigation—that the man she had been working with wasn't an impostor.

"I'll find out what I can for you, Nancy," Carson Drew said. "I'll make some inquiries right away, and I'll call you as soon as I find out anything."

"Great, Dad. And don't worry about us!" Nancy said. "We're being careful, and we really are having a great time."

Just as Nancy hung up, the telephone rang. It was Bess.

"You need to come to Amber's room right away," Bess said.

"What's wrong?" Nancy asked. She was beginning to imagine all kinds of horrible things.

"It's too complicated, Nancy," Bess said, "but what we've just learned changes everything."

"Okay," Nancy said. "I'm on my way."

When Nancy reached Amber's cabin, she found Amber lying on the bed. Bess and George were sitting on the sofa. They all looked stunned.

"Amber wants to tell you something, Nancy," Bess said. "You'd better sit down with us."

Nancy joined her two friends on the sofa. "Okay, Amber, what is it that you want to tell me?"

"Craig wasn't really a detective after all, Nancy," Amber said. "He got this job on the cruise ship so he could steal things from the passengers."

Nancy looked at Bess and George.

"Were you ready for that?" Bess asked.

"No, I wasn't," Nancy said.

"It gets better," George added.

Nancy turned back to Amber. "Let's hear the rest of it," she said.

Amber explained to Nancy how one of Craig's friends had told him what incredible valuables people brought on board cruise ships. The friend was sure that these were mostly people from small towns who saw the cruise ship as a place to show off their expensive clothes and jewels.

Together, Craig and Amber concocted the elaborate Interpol story so that Craig would have what looked like a legitimate reason to sneak around—just in case anyone became suspicious. Amber said Craig was really proud of his Interpol ID because it looked so real.

"I don't understand, Amber," Nancy said. "Where is Craig now?"

Amber shrugged. "Craig's plan was to steal a few big-ticket items right before we docked in Port Huron," Amber said. "I was to rent a car and meet him in front of a restaurant downtown. From there we'd drive south to Detroit, hide out for a few days with some friends of his, then decide where we wanted to end up. I rented the car, drove to the restaurant, and waited. Craig never showed up."

"Why didn't you just leave?" Nancy said. "Why did you come back to the ship?"

"I was telling you the truth about that, Nancy. I really don't have anywhere to go," Amber said. "Everything I own is in this cabin. I thought I'd at least have a place to sleep for a few days until I could decide what to do next."

Nancy shook her head. "This is so bizarre," she said. She stood up and started pacing back and forth. "Amber, if Craig did steal anything from the passengers, it won't be long until the losses are discovered," she said. "We'll have to tell the captain about your part in this crime."

"But he'll throw me off the ship right away if you do that. I'd end up in jail!" Amber cried. "I only agreed to come along because I love Craig and because he thought I'd be a good cover for him."

"Nancy, what if Craig didn't steal anything?" Bess said. "What if he decided it wasn't going to work and then just dumped Amber?"

"I was thinking about that," Nancy said. She looked at Amber. "Okay, we won't say anything to the captain just yet, in case Craig *did* get cold feet and didn't end up stealing anything."

"Maybe he really is a creep, Amber, and he just skipped out on you," George said. "If that's the case, you're much better off."

Amber stood up. "I think I need to take a hot shower and go to bed," she said. "I'd better enjoy these accommodations while I can, because in a few days I'll be on the street."

The girls stood up.

"We'll make sure that doesn't happen," Bess assured her.

Nancy didn't chime in. She wasn't feeling quite as optimistic as her friend.

"If you need anything tonight, just call our suite," George said. "We'll do our best to help you."

"Thank you," Amber said. "I can't even begin to tell you three how much I appreciate what you're doing."

On the way back to their suite George said, "This cruise is getting stranger and stranger."

"That's the truth," Bess said. "I don't know what to think about Amber, Craig, Laura . . ."

"Well, I may have a solution to this in a few minutes," Nancy said. "I called Dad in Toronto and asked him to find out what he could about an Interpol investigation into diamonds stolen from jewelry stores in Mexico and the United States. He should be calling soon." She looked at Bess, who was clearly trying to keep quiet. "Don't say it—I know I should have done it sooner."

As Nancy inserted the key in the lock on their suite's door, the phone rang. She quickly opened the door and grabbed the phone.

"Hello? Oh, hi, Dad!" Nancy said. "Did you find out anything?"

Nancy listened for several minutes, then said, "Well, that does shed some new light on the case."

"Well?" Bess asked after Nancy had hung up.

"There *is* an Interpol investigation of jewelry store robberies," Nancy said, "and the lead investigator *is* a Craig Oliver, but . . ."

"But what?" George said.

"Dad couldn't get a description of him," Nancy said, "so now I don't know if the man we thought was Craig Oliver really *is* Craig Oliver."

12

Overboard!

"Well, if the Craig Oliver we know isn't the real Craig Oliver, then where is he?" Bess said.

"Only the phony Craig Oliver knows that, and he's back in Port Huron," George said. "Right, Nancy?"

Nancy didn't say a word. Bess had to break the silence. "Nancy?" she said.

"Maybe the Craig Oliver we know *is* the real Craig Oliver after all," Nancy said.

"But that would mean that Amber is lying," Bess said, "and I don't think she is."

"She *was* really upset, Nancy," George said. "That didn't seem like an act to me."

"You're right, it didn't," Nancy said. "But how can these two men have the same name?"

"Amber's boyfriend did something with the real

Craig Oliver and took his name," Bess suggested. "Amber only knew him as Craig Oliver."

"That's a possibility. We know there's a Craig Oliver who works for Interpol," Nancy said. "And there's a Craig Oliver who's a petty thief? It's too much of a coincidence. It must be something like you're suggesting, Bess."

"This is confusing, Nancy," George said. "What do you plan to do?"

"Whatever I can. With or without Craig Oliver— whoever and wherever he is—there really is an ongoing investigation," Nancy said. "I'll just turn over any information I uncover to Interpol."

Suddenly, a loud clap of thunder shook their suite.

George walked over to the porthole and looked out. "Where did those storm clouds come from?" she said. "They look really bad."

Nancy and Bess joined George at the porthole.

Nancy frowned. "I hope we pass through this storm before we reach Lake Erie," Nancy said. "These Great Lakes storms are as dangerous as storms on the high seas."

"We must already be in Lake St. Clair," George said. "We still have to go through the Detroit River before we reach Lake Erie."

A brilliant flash of lightning startled them away from the porthole.

After a moment Nancy returned to the porthole. "I think the storm is heading to the southeast," she said. "That'll take it over Canada and then onto Lake Erie." She turned away from the porthole and looked at Bess and George. "Maybe it's moving faster than we are."

"I hope so," Bess said. "I don't like to think about getting seasick."

"Should we try to eat while our stomachs are still in good shape?" George asked.

Bess and Nancy agreed that that was the right idea.

As the girls started to leave the room Nancy said, "Maybe we should call Amber to see if she wants to join us."

"It might make her feel better," Bess said.

"She also might remember some more details that would help Nancy with the investigation," George said.

"True," Nancy agreed. "It would help if she could remember *something* that might lead us to the Craig Oliver who was on the ship."

Bess went over to the telephone and dialed Amber's cabin. She let it ring several times. "She must not be in," she said, hanging up the phone.

"Well, I guess she's not too upset to leave her room," George said.

"She might not be answering," Nancy said. But

somehow Nancy felt that George was right—Amber wasn't there.

Nancy locked the door to the suite, and they headed for the elevator.

When they got to the restaurant, they saw Amber sitting at her table. She seemed engrossed in her food and wasn't paying attention to anyone else.

Laura Houston and the Lowes, on the other hand, were engaged in an animated conversation when Nancy, Bess, and George walked up to the table.

"We were just talking about the storm," Mrs. Lowe said. "Do you think the captain will try to ride it out?"

"I doubt it. He may dock somewhere in the Detroit area if it gets too bad," Mr. Lowe said. "Laura here says she hopes he doesn't, so we won't be delayed."

"I need to get to Canada as soon as possible," Laura said. "I have some business to take care of."

"I'm sure the captain will do what's best for the passengers," Nancy assured Mr. Lowe. "I imagine he's looking at weather maps right now."

"Let's change the subject," Bess said. "I get seasick just talking about storms."

"Good idea," Laura said. She picked up her menu. "What am I going to have tonight?"

For the next several minutes they discussed what was available for the evening meal. Their waiter appeared just as the last person was making her choice.

Soon the conversation shifted to what was happening on the ship. Nancy was surprised that Laura and the Lowes had heard that Craig had not reboarded.

"I understand that his girlfriend is now stranded," Mrs. Lowe said. "I think that's really awful!"

"So do I," Laura said. She looked at Nancy. "Tell us again, how do you know her?"

"We met her at a new boutique in River Heights," Nancy said. "She had never gone on a cruise before, and she wanted some help picking out some clothes."

"Well, this will probably be the last cruise she ever goes on," Mr. Lowe said. "I can't imagine that it's been a pleasant experience for her."

Nancy was trying desperately to think of a way to shift the subject away from Amber, since she didn't want to answer too many questions. She didn't have to worry, though, because just at that moment the ship's horn sounded.

"What's that for?" George asked.

"We've entered Lake Erie. We have one more stop before Toronto: Lake Erie Beach," Laura said. "There are several wonderful small candy factories there. I'm really looking forward to picking up some boxes to take back with me to New Orleans."

"I don't think that any candy can beat those New Orleans pralines," Mr. Lowe said. "They are absolutely delicious."

That started a long discussion of candy. It lasted for almost an hour and made everyone hungry for something sweet.

"I think I'm going to have to stop off at the gift shop before we go back to the cabin," Mrs. Lowe said. "Their candy may not be the best, but it's some—"

Before she could finish the sentence, a loud clap of thunder rocked the boat. It was followed by a brilliant flash of light and a loud crashing sound.

Several passengers screamed.

Mr. Lowe jumped up. "A bolt of lightning must have hit the ship!" he said. He sniffed the air. "I can even smell the lightning. We get a lot of this in Texas."

Just then a voice came over the loudspeaker. "This is your captain. Unfortunately, one of those Great Lakes storms is passing right over us. Please return to your cabins. These generally don't last very long, but the ride will be a bit choppy for a while."

The crew began shepherding the passengers toward the exits. Nancy looked in the direction of Amber's table and saw Amber look around furtively. She got up and headed toward the kitchen.

That's strange, Nancy thought. She pulled Bess

116

and George aside. "Amber just ducked into the kitchen. I'm going to follow her," she said. "You two go on to the suite."

"Okay," Bess said, "but be careful."

"Are you sure you don't need some help, Nancy?" George asked.

"I'll be fine," Nancy said. "I'm just going to see what she's up to."

To get to the kitchen, Nancy had to swim against the tide of people leaving. She managed to make it to the side of the restaurant, where it was a little easier to walk.

"Miss!" one of the crew members shouted at her. "You need to go the other way!"

"I forgot something!" Nancy said to the young man, not giving him time to question her.

Nancy finally reached the swinging doors that led to the kitchen, and she slipped inside.

The kitchen staff was so busy securing utensils and cleaning up food that had spilled that they did not even notice her. As Nancy maneuvered her way through the kitchen looking for Amber, she thought maybe Amber had hidden in the kitchen in order to steal some food. After a quick run through the room, though, Nancy realized that Amber hadn't stayed in the kitchen.

Nancy slipped through a row of sinks filled with dirty dishes and found a rear entrance. When she tried to open the door, it felt as though someone was on the other side, pushing against it. Nancy finally managed to get the door open enough to realize the force of the wind had been pushing the door closed. With a supreme effort, she was able to slip through the door, and she found herself right at the edge of the ship. Only a metal railing kept her from falling into the rough water below.

Suddenly, the ship severely rocked. Another flash of lightning illuminated a huge wave coming right toward her. Nancy tried to open the door again, but it had locked behind her. She grabbed hold of the railing just before she was slammed by the wave.

For several seconds Nancy lost all sense of direction. The force of the water pushed her back toward the door to the kitchen, but she clung to the metal railing with all her might. As the wave washed back off the deck of the ship, it pulled Nancy against the railing. Again, her fingers held tight.

Finally, Nancy was able to stand up—although the ship was still riding the waves at such sharp angles that she was strongly pushed and pulled.

Nancy knew that somehow she had to make it into one of the interior corridors. She had to get away from the fury of the lake.

Nancy slowly made her way around the edge of the ship, sliding her hands along the railing. She tried to recall what she could of the layout of deck 3. She knew the restaurant took up almost a third of it. The kitchen was at one end of the deck. She'd have a ways to go until she could reach a door that would lead to the area where the cabins were located.

Why would Amber have gone this way? Nancy wondered. Surely it wasn't a shortcut to her cabin. Was she planning to meet someone in another cabin? Who could it be?

The boat suddenly tilted to one side, and Nancy found herself slammed against the deck wall. When the ship tilted toward the lake, Nancy almost fell over the railing.

Just as the ship righted itself again and Nancy had started to move slowly along the railing, a hand clamped over her mouth—and another hand started pushing her over the railing.

It took Nancy's brain only a split second to understand what was happening. This had to be the same person who had wanted her to have an accident on the stairs.

Nancy tried to scream, but nothing came out through the person's fingers.

Just then another wave washed over the railing, momentarily freeing Nancy from the person's grip. She slammed onto the deck, and her mouth filled with water. Out of the corner of her eye, she barely made out a hooded figure rushing away.

Nancy began coughing. She was finding it difficult to breathe. She knew that she had to escape, though, or she'd be tossed into the lake.

Slowly, Nancy started crawling along the slippery deck. It was almost impossible to move forward, as the motion of the ship kept forcing her back, but she mustered as much strength as she could. She had to get away from the person who was trying to throw her overboard.

Nancy could feel her fingernails break as she clawed at the deck floor to keep from sliding backward.

Suddenly, strong hands grabbed her from behind, pulled her up, and once again tried to shove her over the side.

Nancy clung desperately to the railing. The ship was now tilting from side to side. Just as Nancy thought she could no longer hold on, the ship tilted so that it forced her attacker back against the wall of what Nancy was sure must be the restaurant. Unfortunately, there were no portholes along this part, so there was no one who could see what was going on.

The ship quickly tilted the other way, and Nancy found herself hanging onto the other side of the railing.

"Help me!" Nancy screamed. "Help!"

But she knew that the storm was making so much noise that no one could possibly hear her cries.

Her attacker was trying to pry her fingers off the railing. Nancy hung on tenaciously. The ship began rocking back and forth even more violently than before. Suddenly, Nancy's fingers slipped off the railing. She began falling.

13

Like Mother, Like Daughter

A pile of lounge chairs on deck 2 broke Nancy's fall. Just as she landed the ship tilted again, so instead of sliding toward the railing, Nancy and the chairs crashed against a wall. Nancy was stunned, but conscious. She struggled to sit up. Nancy knew that whoever had done this might be at that very moment coming down from the deck above to finish the job.

Nancy was feeling sick, and her evening gown was torn in several places. Finally, she got to her feet.

She used the railing to steady herself and tried to make it to safety. Nancy remembered that deck 2 consisted only of cabins. There were no other facilities on it. What she had to do now was get to her suite. At the moment she trusted no one on the ship—except Bess and George, of course. Nancy had no idea who had pushed her over the railing, but the last thing she wanted to do was to make the mistake of asking for help from someone who had just tried to kill her.

Nancy didn't know if it was her imagination or not, but the ship didn't seem to be riding as high on the waves as it had been a few minutes ago. Maneuvering along the railing wasn't very difficult now since no waves were crashing on deck. The thought that the storm might actually be dissipating encouraged her to keep moving.

Finally, Nancy found some stairs that led to the next deck. She looked up, trying to see if the hooded figure was waiting for her at the top. Not seeing anyone, Nancy decided to take a chance. The metal railings were still slippery. She clung tightly to them and slowly made her way up the steps.

When Nancy reached deck 3, she hesitated a second before deciding to use the stairs to reach deck 4. After all, she told herself, her assailant could still be on deck 3. It might be prudent of her to avoid looking for the elevators.

Nancy made it to the next deck without any trouble, but she was beginning to ache all over. She was sure that nothing was broken, but the fall had definitely been a shock to her body—so much so that she wasn't sure she could climb the stairs to deck 5. Although the waves didn't seem overly high, it was still raining quite hard. It took Nancy several minutes to locate a door to the interior, but once she was inside, she rested for a moment. Then she leaned up against the wall and slid her way slowly toward the elevators.

Nancy soon found herself in familiar surroundings. She pushed the elevator button and stepped back, suddenly remembering a scene she had seen in a mystery movie. Someone in a condition similar to hers had been standing right in front of the elevator doors when they opened, and she was immediately grabbed by the person who had been stalking her.

When the doors opened, though, Nancy could see that the elevator was empty. Nancy got on and pushed the button for deck 5. Traveling up, she stood very close to the doors so that when they opened she could get out as quickly as possible.

Nancy's whole body was now throbbing with pain. She slid along the wall of the corridor until she finally made it to her suite. It was then that she realized that the purse she had taken with her to dinner was missing. She was sure that it had washed overboard. It held only her makeup and her cell phone, no important papers or credit cards, so it was no big loss. But it also had her key to their suite—so she had to knock on the door.

Bess immediately flung the door open. "Nancy!" she screamed. "Where have you been? What happened?" Throwing down one of her crutches, she took Nancy's arm and helped her inside. "We tried your cell phone, but we got no answer."

George took Nancy's other arm. "We wanted to go look for you, but the crew said we had to stay in our cabin," she said. "Did they find you?"

Nancy managed to shake her head. She had begun to shiver violently. "Could you get me a blanket?" she whispered. "Hurry." Nancy knew that she was about to go into shock.

Bess and George quickly helped Nancy undress and get into bed. They piled on top of her all the blankets they could find.

For several minutes Nancy continued to shiver uncontrollably. Then she began to warm up. Bess had made some hot tea. She held the cup while Nancy sipped what she could.

Incredibly, the ship was now almost completely stabilized. Lake Erie had almost returned to normal.

"I think we should call the doctor," Bess said. "We need to make sure that you're all right."

Although she was almost sure that she was fine, Nancy didn't protest. "First, though, I need to tell you exactly what happened," Nancy said.

Bess and George listened in stunned silence as

Nancy related how she had been pushed over the railing and had been saved only by landing on some plastic deck chairs. Before Bess and George could say anything, Nancy told them that under no circumstances was the doctor to know the whole story. As far as he or she or anyone else was concerned, Nancy had slipped and fallen on her way back to the cabin. "I'll need to report the loss of my cell phone," she said. "It's probably at the bottom of the lake."

Bess went to the telephone and called the clinic. She was told that the doctor was attending to some other passengers who had suffered minor cuts during the storm but that she'd be there to see Nancy shortly.

"What happened is surely related in some way to the Interpol investigation," Nancy said.

"Whoever did this must still believe that Amber's boyfriend is the real Craig Oliver," George said. "Even though he's no longer on the ship, they must think you're continuing the investigation."

"Right, Nancy!" Bess said. "They got rid of the phony Craig Oliver in Port Huron—thinking he was the real Craig Oliver—and now they're trying to get rid of you."

"Amber just thinks that Craig ran out on her," George said. "She doesn't know that someone thought he was a real Interpol agent."

"Something's not making sense, though," Nancy said. "What happened to the real Craig Oliver? *Our* Craig obviously didn't tell Amber the entire truth about what they were doing. Amber thought the Interpol angle was just that: an angle. It obviously wasn't, though, because there really is an investigation into the jewelry store robberies. Why did Craig choose a real investigation and a real agent's name as a cover—and how did he know about all of it?"

"Maybe he overheard somebody talking about the case and decided to assume the agent's identity," Bess suggested. "We don't even know where Amber's boyfriend worked. Maybe in a police station? Even janitors can pick up tidbits of information there."

Thirty minutes later, as Nancy, Bess, and George were still trying to sort out the maze of information, they heard a knock on the suite door.

A woman with a doctor's medical bag was standing at the door. "I'm Jane Dell," she said with a smile. "I'm here to examine the patient."

As it turned out, Nancy was right. Other than a few bruises, which had already turned black and blue, Nancy was fine. Dr. Dell didn't even ask how Nancy got bumped. It was obvious that she was used to all kinds of accidents during storms on the lakes.

Dr. Dell gave Nancy a couple of pills that she said should help with the pain and told her that if she didn't feel any better in the morning, she should come by the clinic.

"Thank you," Nancy said.

After the doctor left, Nancy, Bess, and George all agreed that the only thing they wanted to do now was go to bed.

Nancy didn't sleep well at all. Over and over, she kept seeing the hooded person who had pushed her over the railing.

At dawn Nancy decided to get out of bed. It was much more difficult than she thought it would be. She could hardly move. She forced herself to a sitting position, slowly put her feet on the floor, and pushed herself into a stand.

Little by little, Nancy made it to the bathroom. She thought a very hot shower might make her feel better.

Thankfully, it did. When she came out of the bathroom, Bess and George were just waking up.

"How do you feel, Nancy?" George asked.

"Better now," Nancy replied, "although when I first got up, I felt as though I had been run over by a truck."

Bess limped over to the porthole, and Nancy was glad to see that she could get around now without the crutches. "I see land," Bess said. "Where are we?"

"That's the New York coast," Nancy said. "The

ship stops at Lake Erie Beach before we go through the Welland Canal to Lake Ontario."

"This is where Laura said those candy factories are," Bess said. "I want to check them out."

"When we see her at breakfast, let's tell her we want to go with her," George said.

The girls dressed and headed to the restaurant. When they got there, only the Lowes were seated at the table.

"Where's Laura?" Bess said. "We thought we'd go to the candy factories with her when we get to Lake Erie Beach."

"We haven't seen her," Mrs. Lowe said.

Over breakfast everyone at the table talked about storms: the one they had just gone through the evening before and several that had hit the Texas Panhandle.

"Mr. Lowe and I aren't getting off the ship here. We don't dock very long—just a couple of hours," Mrs. Lowe said. "We're going to get our luggage ready for Toronto. Once we get through the Welland Canal, we're almost there."

On the way back to their suite Nancy said, "Bess, why don't you call Laura and ask her if we can go with her to the candy factories?"

"Okay," Bess said.

But when Bess tried Laura's room, no one answered. "That's strange," she said as she hung up the receiver. "I wonder if we should check on her."

"Maybe she had another upsetting telephone conversation with her husband and doesn't want to be bothered," George said.

Nancy and Bess agreed that might be the case.

"We won't have time to go to all of the candy factories," Bess said, "but I want to make sure that we go to the one that Laura thinks is the best."

"Well, we could ask some of the people in town to see if there's one that most tourists seem to like the best," George suggested.

"We could do that," Nancy said, "or we could just follow the crowds."

Bess and George looked at each other.

"Leave it to Nancy to come up with the most sensible solution," Bess said.

Within an hour, the ship had docked at Lake Erie Beach. The passengers were once again reminded that the ship would be there only for a couple of hours.

"That's not really a lot of time," Bess complained as she, Nancy, and George headed for the gangway on deck 3.

"Well, it's a small place compared to the other ports of call," Nancy told her.

Just as they reached the top of the gangway Bess spotted Laura at the bottom. She started to shout to her, but Nancy stopped her.

"Let's not press our luck, Bess. She may not want company. But now we don't have to follow the crowds—we can just follow Laura and see which candy factory she goes to," Nancy said. "Once we're inside, if we happen to bump into her, we can gauge her mood."

"That sounds like a good idea," George said. "Maybe she doesn't want any company. I don't want to make a nuisance of myself."

Lake Erie Beach had a few more streets than Nancy had thought it would. George and Nancy—with Bess limping just a little behind them—had to hurry to keep from losing sight of Laura Houston. She quickly turned a corner.

Suddenly, the girls heard, "Hey! Wait for me!"

They stopped and looked around. Amber was running toward them.

"I wonder what this is all about," Nancy said.

Just as Amber had almost reached them she stumbled and slid on the sidewalk, scraping a layer of skin from her knee.

"Ow!" Amber cried. "That hurts."

The girls rushed to her side and managed to get Amber into a sitting position. Nancy took a medicated wipe from the alternate purse she had packed and began cleaning the wound.

"You'll need to have this bandaged when we get back to the ship," Nancy said. "Can you stand up?"

Amber managed to stand, but it was obvious that walking on the leg would be difficult for her if she didn't have some help.

"There's a café just up the street," Bess said. "Why don't we get a table there so we can sit down?"

"Oh, thank you so much," Amber said. "Where were you going?"

"We heard that the candy here is very good," George said. "We were thinking about buying some of it."

"Oh, I'm sorry," Amber said. "If you want to go on, I'll be all right."

"That's okay. You're going to need some help getting back on the ship," Nancy said. "Besides, Bess shouldn't be putting too much weight on her leg." She knew that they'd probably never find Laura now—she would be too far gone. "It wasn't really all that important, just something to do."

When the waitress came, they ordered flavored sodas. They soon learned that this was another specialty of Lake Erie Beach—the waitress told the girls the story.

"Delicious!" Bess pronounced after taking a sip.

Nancy, George, and Amber agreed.

"We probably need to head back to the ship," Nancy said. She looked at Amber. "Do you think you can make it?"

Amber stood up and put some weight on her leg.

"It still hurts," she said, "but if I don't walk too fast, it should be all right."

The girls paid their bill, and the four of them headed toward the ship. Most of the other passengers were on their way back. Nancy kept looking around to see if she might spot Laura, but she didn't see her.

The closer they got to the ship, the slower Amber walked.

"This really hurts," she said. "If I'm going to make it up the gangway, I think I'm going to have to lean on someone."

George volunteered.

When they reached the top, Bess said, "Why don't we go to the clinic first so you can get that scrape bandaged? You don't want it to get infected."

Amber gave a little laugh. "You sound just like my mother," she said. "No, if you'll just take me to my cabin, that'd be great. I have some ointment and some bandages in my suitcase."

"Are you sure?" Nancy said. "It's no problem to stop at the clinic."

"I'm sure," Amber said.

The closer they got to Amber's cabin, the faster Amber seemed to be able to move.

"Have you decided what you're going to do once you get to Toronto?" Nancy asked her.

Amber shook her head. She took her key out of

133

her purse, inserted it in the lock, and opened the door.

The four of them entered the room.

Suddenly, the door slammed behind them. Nancy turned to see Laura Houston pointing a gun at her.

14

Bound and Gagged

"Laura!" Bess cried. "What's going on?"

"Be quiet," Laura said. She turned to Amber. "What happened to your knee? Are you all right?"

"I'm fine, Mother," Amber said. "I scraped it on the sidewalk when I fell."

Mother! Nancy thought.

"You need to be more careful," Laura said. "You won't be much use to me if you can't walk."

Amber's eyes flashed angrily. "I was trying to stop them from following you, Mother!" she said. "I only meant to fake an accident—but I really did trip. Thanks for caring so much!"

"Well, clean it up," Laura said. "It looks awful."

Nancy was just now starting to recover from the stunning discovery about Amber and Laura Houston's relationship. She turned to Amber. "She's your mother?"

Amber looked at her. "Yes. I'm such a lucky girl, aren't I?"

"Keep quiet, Amber," Laura cautioned.

"I'm totally confused," George said.

"So am I," Bess said.

"Why don't you girls have a seat?" Laura said. "You're not going anywhere until we've left the ship in Toronto, so you might as well get comfortable."

Nancy, Bess, and George walked over to the bed on the far side of the cabin and sat down. Nancy noticed several gift boxes of candy stacked in a chair by the bed. Laura had obviously gone to one of the candy factories after all.

"Now, Amber and I have some things to explain to you," Laura said. "Amber, make sure the door is locked."

"Okay, Mother," Amber said. "I see you got the candy for Uncle CN."

Laura laughed. "Yes! He's such a tower of strength, but he still needs his candy!"

Amber removed the boxes of candy from the chair and stacked them on the floor. She then pushed the chair in front of the door to the cabin and sat down.

"What are you going to do with us?" Bess said.

"Don't worry," Laura said. "We're just going to tie

you up so that nobody will find you until we've had time to lose ourselves in Toronto."

Nancy looked at Amber. "I knew when I first saw you in River Heights that you were an athlete," she said. "You're the one who tried to push me overboard last night, aren't you?"

"Well, I do work out with weights, but I wasn't trying to push you overboard," Amber said. "I was only going to put you out of commission for a while." She looked at her mother and rolled her eyes. "What kind of people do they think we are, anyway?"

"Don't ask!" George muttered.

"You stole my canvas bag, didn't you?" Bess said.

Amber nodded. "I wanted to find out more about you three," she said.

"Are you planning any more 'accidents' for us?" Nancy asked.

"No, we've run out of accidents. We'll just have to settle for delaying your departure from the ship so that you can't contact the authorities before we've escaped," Laura said. She grinned at them. "Is that okay?"

Nancy ignored Laura's sarcasm. "How does Craig Oliver figure in to all of this?" she asked.

"Poor, naive Craig Oliver. How he ever became an Interpol investigator, I'll never know. He was so easy to play," Amber said. "I met him accidentally on purpose at a party and let him fall for me so I would be in a position to watch his every move. Mother and I knew he was investigating the jewelry store robberies. You see, we have all kinds of connections in police departments all over the country."

"That's scary," George said.

"Not for us, it isn't," Laura said.

Nancy gave one of the portholes a furtive glance. She could tell that the ship had started through the Welland Canal, which led to Lake Ontario. She had to think fast. They'd soon be in Toronto, and Amber and Laura would escape.

"Somehow Interpol found out that the person behind the robberies—Craig didn't know it was my mother!—was planning to escape from the United States on a Great Lakes cruise ship. Craig got himself hired to help on the ship so he could work undercover," Amber continued. "Of course, Craig told me that the job on the cruise ship was his real job." Amber shook her head in disbelief. "I can play really dumb when I want to. He didn't know that I knew everything about him. I told him that I thought it would be so much fun if I could go on this cruise with him because I had never been on a cruise ship before." Amber laughed. "Craig fell for every line I fed him."

"Where is he now?" Nancy asked.

"He's locked in the basement of an abandoned house in Port Huron," Amber said. "He has enough food and water to survive for a couple of weeks, and by then we'll be buried so deep inside Canada that Interpol will never find us."

"That's terrible," Bess said. "What happens when the food and water run out?"

"One of us will make an anonymous telephone call to the Port Huron Police Department," Laura said. "They'll find him and let him go."

"I don't think Interpol will like it when they discover that one of their agents was tricked into letting the notorious diamond robber escape," Amber said. "It'll probably be the end of his career."

"We can only hope," Laura said, looking at her daughter. "He gave us way too much trouble."

"I'm going to take a shower," Amber said. "Okay?"

"Okay," Laura said. "I'll keep an eye on these three."

"Where's your twin sister?" Nancy said, shooting Bess and George a knowing look.

Laura gave Nancy a dirty look. "You think you're smart, don't you? Well, there's nothing to connect Louise to this operation. She agreed to stand in for me during the first part of the cruise, just to make sure things were safe. I was careful during the robberies, but sometimes you do leave fingerprints without knowing it. If Interpol tried to make an arrest, they wouldn't be able to identify her fingerprints."

Laura was quiet for the next several minutes, but she kept the gun pointed at the girls.

When Amber finally came out of the bathroom, Laura handed her the gun. "Keep an eye on them," she said. "I have to go to my cabin to get the rope."

"Okay," Amber said.

After Laura left the cabin, Amber said, "We're not going to hurt you, really—but please don't try anything. We know what we're doing."

"How could you really know what you're doing if you're involved in something like this?" Nancy said. She looked Amber straight in the eye. "You know, there's still time to get out of it. All you have to do is let us go."

Amber took a deep breath. "I can't do that," she said. "You have no idea what my mother would do to me."

"Look, Amber," George said, "we'd protect you."

Amber started shaking her head. "No! Just keep quiet. I don't want you to say anything else!"

"Please, Amber, just think. . . ," Nancy said.

Just then the door to the cabin opened, and Laura reentered with a paper bag. "What was that shouting all about?" she said. "I could hear you two cabins down."

"Nothing," Amber said.

Laura looked first at Amber then at Nancy. "Good," she said. She walked over and took the gun from Amber.

There goes our chance, Nancy thought.

For the next two hours Nancy had to endure a movie that she had purposely avoided in the theaters. Amber thought it was hysterically funny.

When it was finally over, Laura looked out the porthole and said, "That's Toronto in the distance, so it's time to tie you girls up."

Nancy thought perhaps the crew would discover them before Laura and Amber had a chance to leave the ship, but Laura shattered that hope.

"We're going to put you in the bathroom so that when they come to get our luggage, no one will know you're here," Laura said. She gave them a big smile. "And in case you're thinking that some of the crew will come along, checking the cabins after we're gone, forget it. Oh, they check the cabins all right, but Amber has been complaining about how difficult it is to open her door—so right before we leave, we're going to fix the lock so that it won't open with a key. The door itself will have to be removed. That won't happen until later today at the earliest, and we'll be long gone."

"What about our suite?" Bess said. "The crew will notice that we haven't left the ship and will come looking for us."

"No, they won't. Passengers are given two hours after docking before they have to get off the ship," Laura said. "So, disguising my voice as George's— since I knew they hadn't talked to her as much as they had talked to you and Nancy—I called Guest Services and told them that the three of you wanted to wait until the last minute to leave."

"I see you've thought of everything," Nancy said.

"Of course," Laura said. "That's why I'm able to carry several millions of dollars' worth of diamonds into Canada without anyone ever guessing how I'm doing it."

15

Sweet, Sweet Diamonds

Laura had tied Nancy's hands behind her, so she couldn't see her watch. She wasn't sure how long they had been in the bathroom when she suddenly heard a loud noise coming from somewhere near Amber's cabin.

With duct tape over their mouths, it was impossible to communicate with one another—and Nancy hadn't really tried, thinking that her father would eventually insist on a thorough search of the ship. Of course, the more time that elapsed before that happened, Nancy knew, the less likely it was that Laura and Amber would be caught.

All of a sudden, Nancy heard a crashing sound, as though . . . Yes! It had to be the door to the cabin falling onto the floor. The crew had done exactly what Laura said they would: remove the door.

Nancy tried to send a message to Bess and George with her eyes: *Start kicking the walls of the bathroom.* She looked at their legs and then quickly looked at the door.

Bess and George understood. The three of them began kicking as hard as they could.

A voice near the bathroom door called out, "Nancy!"

Nancy's hopes soared. Her father had found them!

Within seconds, the bathroom door opened. Sure enough, Carson Drew was standing next to a member of the ship's crew. There was also a third person with her father whom Nancy hadn't expected to see: Craig Oliver.

The three men quickly took the duct tape off the girls' mouths and untied them.

"What are you doing here?" Nancy asked Craig as she massaged her wrists to restore the circulation.

"It's a long story, Nancy," Craig said. "Where's Amber?"

"She left the ship with her mother," Nancy said.

Craig blinked. "Her mother? What are you talking about?"

"Laura Houston is Amber's mother. She is the one who's responsible for all those jewelry store robberies in Mexico and the United States," Nancy explained. "Amber knew all about it."

"Well, I knew Amber was in on it," Craig said, "but I never suspected that it was her *mother*. I thought it might be a father or a brother—or a boyfriend." He let out a big sigh. "I wouldn't have been looking for a woman leaving the ship—and Amber probably had on a disguise."

"I thought *you* were her boyfriend, Craig," Bess said.

"It's all very complicated, and Craig can explain it to you later," Mr. Drew said. "What we need to do now is find those two. Nancy, do you have any idea where they went?"

"I think I do," Nancy said. "The CN Tower?"

"Well, we're in luck," Craig said. "It's right on Lake Ontario, just a few blocks from here. Come on."

"What about our things?" Bess said. "I have a lot of new clothes!"

"That's all taken care of," Mr. Drew said. "The cruise company is making sure that all of your things are taken to the Queen Elizabeth Hotel."

The five of them hurried down the gangway as fast as Bess could maneuver on her bad ankle and headed to the car that Mr. Drew had driven to the dock.

"How did you know the CN Tower was where they were going?" Mr. Drew asked as they got into the car.

"It was something Amber and Laura said to each other, Dad," Nancy said. "I'll explain when we get there."

On the way to the CN Tower, Craig said, "I'm sure you're wondering about me."

"I certainly am," Nancy said.

"Well, I couldn't tell you everything, Nancy—but I did tell you as much as I could," Craig began.

It turned out that Craig knew all about Amber's plan from the start. "In fact, I set myself up," he said. "I purposely played the naive investigator."

"You certainly did a great job," Nancy said. "I couldn't believe that Interpol would really have someone as naive as you working for them."

Craig laughed. "I was wrong about the fugitive, though. She didn't fit the profile."

"Well, maybe profiling doesn't always work," George said.

"Touché!" Craig said. "Amber put something in my iced tea at the restaurant, and the next thing I knew, I woke up in that abandoned house in Port Huron."

"How did you get out?" Nancy asked.

Craig pointed to his watch. "It has a transmitter in it. Interpol always knows where I am. When I didn't call in at my normal time, they located me. I decided that the best strategy from there would be to meet Amber and whomever she was with when the ship docked in Toronto. I thought they'd think that it was still safe to carry out their planned operation. When I arrived at the dock, I saw your father. I recognized him from television interviews and pictures I've seen in newspapers. I introduced myself, and he told me you had called him about the investigation. As I said, Amber must have been disguised or she saw me talking to your father . . . or something. In any case, she slipped past me. When the three of you didn't disembark, we both knew that something was wrong. After we looked in your suite, I decided that you might be in Amber's. We had to take the door off the hinges to get it open—and that's when we knew you'd be inside."

"Right—Amber and her mother disabled the lock," Nancy said. "They had this all planned out."

They soon arrived at the CN Tower on Front Street. Mr. Drew parked the car.

"Wow!" George exclaimed. "That is one tall building."

"It's the tallest freestanding structure in the world," Mr. Drew said.

As they headed inside the building Craig said, "There are four lookouts near the top of the tower, but if I were going to meet someone to exchange stolen merchandise, I think I'd choose 360. That's the revolving restaurant near the top of the tower."

Craig's Interpol identification card got them to the

head of the line for one of the express elevators. They whizzed up over 1,000 feet within seconds.

When the elevator doors opened, Nancy immediately spotted Laura and Amber. They were at one of the tables across the room. A man was sitting opposite them.

"That's Piet Van Rooyen, a South African diamond dealer," Craig said. "He's at the top of Interpol's most-wanted list."

The five of them stepped out of the elevator and stood to one side, where they would be out of Laura and Amber's line of vision.

"Nancy," Craig said, "how did you know they'd be here?"

"Laura picked up several boxes of candy in Lake Erie Beach when the ship stopped there," Nancy explained. "When we got to Amber's room—we fell for her accident onshore, and helped her back to her suite—Laura was waiting for us there with the candy and a gun. Amber mentioned that the candy was for Uncle CN, and Laura said that even though he was a tower of strength, he still needed his candy. I just picked up on the key words."

"But that doesn't explain where the diamonds are," Craig said.

"Oh, yes it does," Nancy said. "Ever try chocolate-covered diamonds?"

"Oh, my gosh!" Bess exclaimed. "You're kidding."

"No, I'm not," Nancy said.

"What a perfect hiding place," George said.

"Well, I can't be positive that that's where the diamonds are, but it certainly makes sense," Nancy said. "What look like chocolate-covered clusters of nuts could easily be millions and millions of dollars' worth of chocolate-dipped diamonds!"

"Amazing!" Craig said, looking at Nancy. He took out his cell phone and made a quick call. "The Toronto authorities have been waiting to hear from me," he said. "They'll be the ones making the arrests. We'll stay here, though, until they arrive."

Five minutes later all of the elevators to the 360 Restaurant opened up, and swarms of Toronto police officers burst into the room. Craig led the officer in charge of the operation over to Laura and Amber's table.

"I think this would be an appropriate time to show ourselves," Nancy whispered to Bess and George.

They moved away from the bank of elevators and into the middle of the room. Amber saw them immediately. She whispered something to her mother, and Laura looked in their direction.

Nancy could only imagine what was going through their minds. They were probably wishing now that Nancy had fallen into Lake Erie instead of onto the deck chairs.

Nancy watched as Laura, Amber, and Mr. Van

Rooyen slowly stood up to be handcuffed by the Toronto police.

Craig picked up the boxes of chocolate and came back to where Nancy, her friends, and Carson Drew were standing.

"One of the boxes was open," Craig said, showing them the container. "Look. You can see a small sparkle in the chocolate! I guess Mr. Van Rooyen wanted to make sure that this chocolate wasn't full of nuts."

"With those two, you can't be too careful," George said. "I kind of don't blame him!"

"I have to go with the police," Craig said. "Thanks for all your help, Nancy. You'll be hearing from me soon." He turned to Bess and George. "I also appreciate what you two did."

"I'm glad everything worked out all right, Craig," Nancy said. "I feel better knowing that you really did have this investigation under control."

Craig grinned at her. "Well, for the most part," he said. "But I now know to be less of a stickler about profiling when I'm on certain cases!"

Craig followed a couple of the Toronto police officers onto one of the elevators, and the doors closed behind them.

"Well!" Carson Drew said. "That was quite an ending to your Great Lakes cruise, hmm?"

Nancy and her friends laughed.

"How about we eat?" Mr. Drew said.

"Definitely!" Bess said.

As they followed the maître d' to their table Nancy finally felt herself relaxing. Maybe now she could start to enjoy their vacation.

"This is the best view in the restaurant," the maître d' said, pulling out Nancy's seat.

"Great," Nancy said. "Thanks!"

"Oh no, Nancy! Look!" Bess gasped. "I thought I'd never have to see that again!"

Nancy and George moved closer to the window to see what Bess was pointing at. Below them, like a toy ship floating in a puddle of water, was the SS *Great Lakes*.

"Is there a problem?" the maître d' asked. "I can seat you somewhere else."

"Oh, no, I'll just change places with her," Nancy said.

"All right," the maître d' said. "Your waiter will be with you momentarily."

"With everything that happened to you on that ship, Nancy," Bess said, "I'd think you'd never want to see it again either."

"They're not all bad memories, Bess," Nancy assured her.

"Well, that's good to hear," Mr. Drew said. "For a while I thought I had made a mistake by sending you girls on the cruise."

"Don't forget, Bess, that ship was the setting for one of Nancy's greatest cases," George said, quickly adding, "*and* I made a new friend: Brad Snider." She grinned. "Oh, and did I fail to mention that I got everyone tickets to his first preseason game?"

Bess's eyes widened. "You didn't. Did you?"

While Bess and George started making plans for that upcoming event, Nancy looked out the window at the SS *Great Lakes*. This far up, everything that had happened to her in the last few days seemed like a dream—or, more accurately, a nightmare!

Slowly, Nancy allowed her eyes to scan the rest of the Toronto landscape. *Is there another mystery waiting for me down there?* she wondered.

She decided that if there was, it could just wait—because right now she was hungry!